# DEATH WAITS FOR NO LADY

*a historical murder mystery set in Yorkshire*

## JAMES ANDREW

10·09·19

THE
BOOK
FOLKS

Paperback published by The Book Folks

London, 2019

ISBN  978-1-7942-4594-5

www.thebookfolks.com

*To Jennifer*

# CHAPTER ONE

A scratching somewhere woke him, and he tried to place the noise, then realised it must be a branch against the bedroom window. He blinked as his eyes took in the grey of dawn before he glanced at the dark, curly head beside him. He was pleased to see that Jean still slept. He tried to suppress a groan as he turned onto his other side to avoid the creep of light. He thought perhaps this would help his sleep return, but the branch still knocked, and his mind returned to that blood-sodden place it often was at this time of day. He possessed a high-sounding title, Inspector Stephen Blades of Yorkshire Constabulary, but, when waking, he was often a quaking wreck as he thought again of that blood-soaked sand, and that rock.

His eyes began to concentrate on his surroundings. This bedroom reflected Jean, with that framed picture of a sunny meadow and those rose-patterned curtains, and he thought of the neatness with which clothes were arranged in drawers and hung in wardrobes. He was sure that if she did not have him so calmly organized, he would never get through anything; he was glad to be reassured by the steady sound of her breathing as she slept.

His mind filled again with the rush of waves on the shore and he could still feel the coolness of the breeze on his skin as he had stood on the sand gazing at the body on the blood-drenched sand, its auburn-locked head gashed by a rock. This had been the third corpse on that beach in a few months and, as one of the investigating officers, he still felt responsible. They should have caught the murderer before then.

Blades turned to his other side, then back again, realised sleep was not returning, and rose, pulled on his dressing gown, then staggered to the bathroom where he relieved himself. As he started on his morning wash, he reflected that the grey, anxiety-ridden face in the mirror was almost unrecognizable as his own.

The murders had stopped. They never knew why, just as they had never found out who had committed them, and Blades still wondered whether he deserved to continue in his job. It was Chief Inspector Walker of Scotland Yard who had been in charge, with Blades seconded onto the investigating team for his local knowledge. After the investigation, Walker had been moved from the Yard to one of the local forces. Blades had felt the disgrace as well, but they had praised his conscientiousness. Blades supposed that one scapegoat was considered enough, he had continued with normal duties and hoped no major crimes would come along. He attempted to look sure of what he was doing although he no longer was.

Blades was tall and wide-framed, with a strong jaw and, normally, a naturally firm look in his eyes; he had a reasonably quick brain, and possessed a bluffness in his manner which helped inspire confidence in others, so that, by putting one foot in front of another with contrived boldness, he got from the beginning of one day's work to the end with surprising lack of incident and sometimes success. But he never forgot he had helped hang an innocent man.

After finishing his toiletries, he gave the mirror a grimace which he corrected into the confident smile it was supposed to be, then walked into the kitchen to put the kettle on for tea. He discovered Jean there ahead of him, yawning and filling it with water ready to be heated.

# CHAPTER TWO

Mary was fourteen and had been in her job as parlour-maid for only a few months. As she had been brought up in a smoke-blackened tenement, she was in awe of the house she found herself working in. Elmwood Hall was one of the best houses in Birtleby, with a seemingly endless number of rooms, and imposing bay windows that looked out over sweeping grounds which, as might be expected, were leafy with elm. The house required an endless amount of work from servants: Mary's day lasted fifteen hours. She thought of herself as less of a parlour-maid and more of a skivvy. Janet had told Mary that fifteen hours had always been normal for a parlour-maid in that house, though what did make things more difficult was that there were fewer servants than there used to be. And even though the staff had been reduced after Miss Wright's father died, Miss Wright expected the house to be kept to the same standard.

It was one of Mary's duties to polish furniture, which included the mahogany wardrobes, the four-poster bed in her lady's room, the escritoire, and the bookcases, among many other pieces. Then there was the silver to be looked after, the cutlery service, the dinner service, the trays, and the silver-framed mirrors and candlesticks. This was on top of the normal housework she had anticipated, the scrubbing of floors and the beating of carpets. Mary had to learn the names of a lot of the furniture she looked after, and she still had no idea what some of the cutlery could be for. There was so much to learn for a girl who had been brought up in two rooms with only a kitchen table and some chairs in one room and, in the other, a 'set-in' bed, a couple more chairs, and a blanket box. Entering service had been walking into a different world, and she had met different types of people there. Her mistress's vowels had been as polished as she expected the silver to be. This was a world of backs held straight, and restricted displays of emotion. Miss Evelyn Wright was the first lady Mary had met and she still had not adjusted to her.

That morning, Mary had started at six, cleaning and blackening the kitchen range and lighting it, then whitening the front steps, and now she was clearing out and making fires in the rest of the house. Because she was doing the dirtier tasks, she was wearing one of her print dresses with a 'morning apron' of rough hessian, though she wore the usual goffer cap. Mary's mother had scrimped and saved for Mary's uniforms. The house was dark, and Mary drew back curtains and lit gas mantles as she went along. When she opened the drawing-room door, light filled it from the hallway so that when she entered that room she could see clearly, too clearly. She shrieked. She dropped the bucket she was carrying. Though this spilled ash over the floor, that did not merit a glance from her. She stood stock still, unable to move.

Stretched out on the Turkish rug in front of the black marble fireplace lay Mary Cunningham's employer, Miss Evelyn Wright, or what had been her. The head was thrown back, bruised and bloody, with the still eyes protruding. There was a wound on her forehead and her nose was at an odd angle. The dark-green georgette dress was bloodied too. Mary stared at Miss Wright's emerald brooch which still sparkled – it seemed incongruous now. Mary gawped at her employer for a further long moment, before she forced herself into the only action she could think of and scurried off to fetch the housekeeper.

Mary had met death before. She had lost a brother in infancy, and a sister had died of TB, but this was her first acquaintance with murder. She was moving in different circles now.

# CHAPTER THREE

As Inspector Blades stepped out of his car outside Elmwood Hall, he noted the elms, the yew hedge, and the ornate iron gates.

'Bit of a change from the type of places we're usually called out to,' his sergeant, Aloysius Peacock, said.

'Sometimes you state the obvious,' Blades replied. 'It's one of the most desirable areas in Birtleby.' And definitely a better class of murder than the last one, he thought, as his mind returned to it. 'I don't suppose it makes any difference to the victim,' he said.

As Blades and his sergeant strode up the drive to the door of the three-storied mansion, Blades glanced at the man beside him. Peacock belied his name with his flat grey cap and grey suit made of a material of questionable quality, and Blades was aware of his own rumpled suit and well-worn bowler. If he had known, he could have put on a dinner jacket.

The door was opened for them by a maid in her teens, who they were to learn was called Mary Cunningham. Her face seemed to be competing with the whiteness of her cap, and the deep-brown eyes gazed at them with anxiety. Blades showed his card as he introduced himself.

'Thank you for coming,' she said, then paused. 'Thank you so much. Please come in.'

They were ushered into the hallway, the servant disappeared, and a buxom, middle-aged lady appeared and introduced herself as Janet Farrell, the housekeeper.

'It's good to see you,' she said. 'We've been beside ourselves. That such a thing should happen, and to such a person. Miss Wright was quality. And I've known her most of her life, girl and woman. I remember her sitting dressing her dolls. I never expected her to meet her end like this.' Then the words seemed to stop by themselves as she stood wringing her hands. 'It's a tragedy.' She stood for another moment, then more words rushed out. 'You'll want to see where she died? Not that I can bear going there again, but we'd better get on with it.'

'If you could show us there, we'd be grateful,' Blades replied.

Janet unlocked the dining room door.

'We haven't disturbed anything,' she said. 'Who would want to, and who would dare? Poor Miss Wright.'

'Thank you,' Blades said as they entered. Both Blades and Peacock peered round.

'And no one's been in at all since the body was discovered?'

'No.'

Blades looked at the corpse prostate on the rug, which suggested Evelyn had been standing in front of the fire when she was killed. He took in the angle of the head, arms and legs, and the position of the blows to the head. It was convenient to see what he took to be the murder weapon –a long-handled, brass, blood-spattered poker –on the rug beside her. Blades' eyes continued round the scene. There was a book on the side-table by the settee and he supposed Evelyn had spent part of the evening reading it. Blades glanced across at Peacock as he saw him nod towards a glass on the mantlepiece, and Blades took in the one on the side-table as well. The glass on the side-table still held some port, though what had been in the one on the mantlepiece had been finished. Plates with sandwiches lay on a large table. All of this suggested someone known and welcomed into the home, and Blades wondered who it could have been. Signs of a struggle were obvious: a lamp and chair had been overturned. There was no indication of the theft of valuables, with items such as Miss Wright's jewellery untouched. Blades supposed there had been an argument, and he wondered at the cause of it. He noticed the lid of the desk was open and wondered if it had revolved around papers. He began by asking Janet his standard questions.

'Do you see anything missing from the room?'

Janet's eyes flicked about the drawing room. 'No.'

'Is there anything you wouldn't expect to see?'

Janet's eyes scanned the room again. 'No.'

That did not mean the visitor had left nothing of himself behind and Blades would make sure he found anything there was, fingerprints at least.

'I take it Miss Wright didn't smoke cigars?' Peacock said. He looked in the direction of an ashtray.

Blades smiled to himself. No. Peacock wouldn't miss that.

'Oh, no, sir.'

'Who was her visitor?' Blades asked.

'Mr Russell, the minister.'

'And there was no one else?'

'No.' Blades noticed the effect the implications of that had on Janet.

'Did you see him when he arrived?'

'I opened the door to him, and I wish I hadn't now,' she said, gazing at the body. Her thoughts seemed to wander, then her face crumpled, and Blades waited for her to recover composure. 'It would have been about eight,' she said at last. 'Miss Wright was expecting him and had me make cucumber sandwiches especially for him.' She gestured to the table with its plates of food and decanter of port. 'Mr Russell did visit sometimes; she said he was a comfort to her after the death of her father, and she didn't like to be disturbed once I'd shown him up. But surely it wouldn't be the minister?'

'We consider anyone and everyone.'

Janet wrung her hands again. 'It does look bad. Digby comes to visit and when someone next enters this room, Miss Wright's lying there dead. Who else could it have been?'

'If the evidence points to him, then it does look bad,' Blades said, 'though it might not continue to. We'll see. About what time did Digby arrive?'

'Let's see. About seven.'

'And could you say what time he left?'

'No, sir. I couldn't.'

Blades turned to Peacock. 'You'd better get the camera out and take the necessary photographs of the crime scene, the body, of course, the glasses, the table with sandwiches, and the open escritoire to start with.'

'Yes, sir.' Peacock set down his black leather bag, took out his bulky camera with its conspicuous flash bulb, and began.

'He was often round,' Janet said. 'She was in a right state after her father died. I didn't think much of him myself. It would have been better if it had been the Methodist minister they always had to do with before, but she'd taken up with the Spiritualist church. I don't believe in all those séances they go in for, but Miss Wright was convinced. And it seemed to help.'

As Blades considered this, he noticed Janet's eyes hardly left the body, and it occurred to him she might be able to think more clearly if she was elsewhere. 'We need to leave Sergeant Peacock to the crime scene,' he said. 'Is there somewhere we can discuss this?'

Janet took him into the dining room. The room was dominated by the well-polished mahogany dining table, its high-backed chairs with their velvet seats, and by a resplendent chandelier. Blades pulled out seats for himself and Janet. Seating himself opposite her, he smiled in as reassuring a manner as he could. She looked taken aback at his self-confidence in Miss Wright's dining room as she seated herself opposite him.

'A dreadful shock for you,' he said.

'Yes, sir.'

'We'll do our best to find your mistress's killer.'

'Thank you, sir.'

'You heard nothing untoward, no loud voices, or the sound of a struggle?'

'No. Come to think of it, I didn't even show him up.' Another anxious look came over her face as if she thought she had been derelict in her duties. Then she continued, 'He's been here so often before.'

'Quite,' Blades said.

'I opened the door to him and he went straight upstairs, and he was just normal. Relaxed and smiling, his smarmy self.' She gave an apologetic-looking smile as if embarrassed by the comment.

'He was?'

'Oh, he's charming. Too much so in my book, but I wouldn't have said so to Miss Evelyn.'

'And where were you during his visit?'

'I was doing accounts in the housekeeper's office.'

'Which is situated where?'

'In the basement.'

'Well away from here. What time did Mr Russell leave?'

'I couldn't tell you. I wasn't listening for him. He always showed himself out.'

'Who found the body?'

'Mary.'

'Could I speak with her?'

Janet walked over to a bell pull beside the fireplace and rang for the maid. When Mary reappeared, Blades studied her. Mary was thin and underdeveloped, and he supposed her background had been impoverished. He hoped life in service would fatten her up a bit. She still looked as anxious as when he had first seen her, with a remarkable number of lines on her forehead for such a young face.

'You found the body?' Blades asked, and Mary nodded.

'It was a shock, sir. I was just coming into the drawing room to do the fire, and there she was. Miss Wright was a proper lady. Who'd have thought anyone would do her in? I can't credit it. I saw her just the day before and she was so full of life.'

'What was she doing when you last saw her?'

'What she did every morning: her piano practice. She did it regularly as clockwork and it was lovely.' Her face looked sad as she said this.

'What was your relationship like with your employer?'

Janet answered for Mary. 'Mary's only been here a few months so she's still settling in, but she got on all right with her.'

'Is there anything you want to add to that?' Blades asked Mary.

'There isn't anything else she can tell you,' Janet said.

'Can't she tell me herself?' Blades asked.

'I'm sorry,' Janet said. 'I shouldn't have interrupted but she's only a girl, and Miss Wright had very little to do with Mary. The mistress saw Mary on the day she arrived when she had her interview with her, but Mary gets all her instructions from me. If Miss Wright had a comment to make about the work Mary was doing, that was made through me.'

'How old are you?' Blades asked Mary.

'Fourteen, sir.'

Mary could have passed for twelve, Blades thought. Still, fourteen was young, even though it was the usual age girls started in service.

'I got on all right with her, when I did see her. Not that she said anything much, as Janet said.'

Blades studied Mary. 'All right,' he said. 'Did you see Mr Russell last night?'

'No. It was my evening off and I didn't come back till ten.'

'Did you see or hear anything then?'

'We use the back entrance and stair, sir. I wouldn't see anything that was going on at this end of the house.'

'And you didn't?'

'No.'

Blades thought he had probably asked Mary enough questions for now but did not dismiss her. He looked across at Janet. 'When was the last time you saw your employer?'

Janet considered. 'She came down to compliment me on her meal. It was some time after six. Then she discussed the next day's menus.'

'And how did she seem?'

'Her normal self. Nothing seemed to be bothering her.'

'How long have you worked for her?'

Janet gave a long, drawn-out sigh. 'About thirty-five years.'

'A fair whack of time.'

'I started here when I was twelve.'

'So, you'll know everything there is to know about Miss Wright?'

'She was a lady from a fine family, and she was a good soul. I felt sorry for her.'

'Why?'

'Her father was a self-centred Tartar and he clung onto Miss Wright so much after her mother died. She was a fine-looking woman, Miss Evelyn, and she had a way with her, so that we thought she would make someone a good catch, but her father saw off any young man who came to call. He wanted her all to himself.'

'How did she react to that?'

'How could she? It's not as if she'd any independent money. Her mother arranged soirées so that Evelyn could be introduced to eligible young men. There was one we thought might have won her, a well set-up gentleman, Alex

Forsyth, from one of the wealthiest families in Birtleby, but Miss Evelyn's father set a private detective on him and found out he'd fathered a baby to another woman, so he forbade Evelyn from seeing him, which might have been fair enough. She'd have finished with him herself when she found that out about him, but it was the same with every young man who came to call. Mr Wright would make a point of finding out any faults or secrets, and make sure Evelyn knew. And who's perfect?'

'Quite.'

'After Evelyn's mother died, the soirées came to a halt, so her father had no more young gentlemen to see off, and he ended up with what he'd decided he wanted, which was Evelyn all to himself. But Evelyn adapted to it. She did her good works on different charity committees – and comforted herself with her piano. She was never away from that. It was as if tinkling away on it was the only way she could express herself. And it was lovely to listen to.'

'Then her father died?'

'He was ill and became a bed-bound invalid for a long time, when he needed her even more, so she got even less of a life then.'

'Did you like him?'

'As an employer? He was no better or worse than any of his class, and who are we servants to criticise them? But, as a father, he was too domineering with Evelyn.'

'So how was she after her father's death?'

'Grief-struck. I thought she became a bit too fond of her own company.'

'Then she found herself a young man, this Digby Russell?'

'If he was her young man. He was her minister and a queer fish. He talks to the dead and gets everyone to believe him.'

'Not a light-hearted, pleasure-loving young man?'

'I wish she'd met one of those. Digby has a light-hearted way with him, but his eyes aren't light.'

'What do you mean?'

'It's hard to say. It's as if he knows something clever no one else does, if that's it.'

'Is he ill-tempered at all?'

'He's charm itself. Some people talked about him and Evelyn because of the number of times he came around – and he was fifteen years younger than her. I thought if she did have a young man it would be a good thing. A bit of life was what she needed.' Then Janet paused as if struck by a thought. 'Not that a bit of life's what she got.'

Blades noticed the poignancy but was aware he couldn't allow himself to indulge it. Fortunately, Janet recovered her composure quickly. 'Do you think there was a romance there?' he said, with a gentle tone.

'It was all kept proper but who's to say?'

Blades waited to see if Janet would elaborate but she did not. 'Do you know anything about enemies Miss Wright might have had?'

'I don't know of anyone she might have disagreed with this much.'

'Who did she have disagreements with?'

'Not that anybody springs to mind at all. She was a good-natured soul.'

Blades looked carefully at Janet. 'How did you find Miss Wright to work for?'

'It was an old-fashioned family. They kept their distance from you. They thought you wouldn't do your work properly otherwise, and Miss Wright was just the same as her father and mother. They'd have preferred it if a maid had been invisible. Mary's work had to be done when Miss Wright wasn't in the room. And Mary had never to show her back to her. Sometimes it meant leaving a room backwards. I don't know how much you know of the ways of big houses, but that's not uncommon.'

'I've some idea. My mother was a housekeeper before she married, and she told us stories about it.'

Janet looked surprised. 'Where was your mother in service?'

'To the Lyons over at Fanthorpe. She was the housekeeper. She married the local grocer she did business with and left.'

'Good for her,' Janet said. A look that Blades couldn't quite place appeared in her eyes, then left. 'Janet's not my name, you know.'

'Isn't it?'

'It's what they always called the housekeeper in that family so it's what they called me. Elizabeth's my real name. Betty. Not that I'd probably answer to it now.' She laughed briefly. 'I came from an orphanage.'

'You did?'

'So I didn't mind. They were being ever so good to us in that establishment, so they said. All the girls were trained for employment, so they would be able to make their own ways in the world, and it was service they trained you for. I wouldn't have minded meeting someone like your mother did, but it was difficult. They didn't approve of followers.'

That look reappeared on her face, then just as quickly vanished again.

'But I've always had a roof over my head – till now. And the Wrights were always decent people to work for.'

'I expect you'll find somewhere soon enough.'

'Maybe. I'm not getting any younger.'

'Was Miss Wright an only child?'

'She had a brother. Not that he had anything to do with the business either.'

'The business?'

'The Wright family. They owned Wright's Biscuits. You'll know of them.'

'Oh, definitely, though I wasn't sure whether Evelyn Wright was part of that family. They've that big factory outside Birtleby?'

'That's where the wealth came from, but the father sold it after he'd grown a bit older and got used to the fact his son wasn't interested.'

'Where does the son live now?'

'Andrew has a place in Harrogate. He and Evelyn kept up with each other though I couldn't say when he was last here, a month or so I suppose. His father settled money on him as he said he felt a man should have independence, so Andrew leads a leisured life, and he writes novels which are supposed to be well thought of, though I've never read them.'

'A brother?' Blades said. 'We'll make sure he's informed. He and his sister were on good terms when they last met?'

'Reasonable. It was a brother and sister relationship. They knew each other inside out and weren't slow to criticise. Andrew didn't think much of Digby. That might be why he hasn't been near the place so much.'

'Where does Digby Russell live?'

Janet told him.

'You and Mary were the only servants?'

'There's the kitchen maid, Katy, and a gardener, Charlie Falconer. He has a cottage in the grounds.'

'Katy?'

'She helps me in the kitchen. She's been here longer than Mary. She came here about a year and a half ago. She was the parlour-maid and then, after Mary came, she was promoted to the kitchen.'

'Was Katy here last night?'

'She had cleaning up to do but she'd have finished about nine. She'd have been up in her room after that. Not that her room's anywhere near where Miss Wright was. The maids are right at the top of the house. And the kitchen's in the basement. She couldn't have heard or seen anything.'

'Still, she'll need to confirm that. And there's a gardener, you say? Would he have been around the house at that time of night?'

'No.'

Although he might have seen someone in the gardens, Blades reflected. He would question him, but not just now.

'Can I talk to Katy?' Blades said.

Janet walked to the bell rope and pulled it again. Blades supposed that everyone was summoned by the clanking of that bell in this house.

A well-developed girl appeared, frowned at Mary, glanced apprehensively at Janet and stared at him. Blades guessed she would be no more than sixteen but, with her build and self-confidence, looked older. Her maid's uniform neither succeeded in disguising her voluptuous figure nor in dampening what looked like a fiery spirit, Blades thought, as he studied the imperious and questioning eyes. But there was some measure of nervousness there and a paleness of the skin that suggested the shock she, like everybody else in this household, must have felt.

He attempted to give her a reassuring smile. 'Inspector Blades,' he said. 'I'm investigating your mistress's death.' Then he paused, wondering how he should proceed. 'Did you hear or see anything untoward?' he said.

'I've enough to do in that kitchen without paying any attention to what's going on upstairs.'

There was a boldness in the reply that made him think this girl might be less nervous than he had expected. 'I suppose not,' he said. 'Though if you'd heard your mistress screaming because someone was attacking her you would have?'

Her veneer of self-composure was rocked at this and her reply gushed out. 'I would then.'

'What time did you finish in the kitchen?'

Now Blades noted that although she met his eyes fully, she shifted from one foot to the other. 'About nine – and then my time was my own, so I wouldn't be looking for Miss Wright in case she gave me something else to do. I just wanted to get my feet up.'

'So you went upstairs to your room?'

'That's right.'

'That wouldn't take you past the drawing room?'

'We go up the back stairs,' Katy replied but did not elaborate.

'I suppose you do.'

'I understand you've been working here about a year and a half?' Blades asked her.

'Yes, sir.'

'And how do you find it here?'

Katy glanced across at Janet. 'It's a good place. Lots of girls my age in service would be jealous of me.'

'You were here when Mr Wright was still alive?'

'Oh yes.'

There was a pause as Blades gave her the opportunity to continue.

'He was a bit of a tyrant with Miss Evelyn, I thought. He treated her as if she were one of the servants. He had her waiting on him hand on foot, but he was as could be expected with us. We are servants.' At this, she suppressed a laugh.

Then Janet interjected. 'She was swallowed up by her father. It was a shame. He could be a selfish man. I knew what she felt.'

'You did?' Blades replied as Katy turned her head to look at Janet with a surprised curiosity. 'What do you mean?' Blades asked.

Janet, who had not looked as if she intended to elaborate, now did, after a moment's hesitancy. 'My sister died.'

'She did?'

'It was cancer and when she was nearing the end of her illness, I wanted to go to her.' She struggled with the thought. 'They don't mean harm, people of this class, but they don't really see you if you're a servant. They think they do right by you, but they don't always. It was all right, Mr Wright said. I could go to my sister if she was ill. But I had to have my duties done first. And there were visitors that weekend and there was all the organizing to do; by the time they'd left, and I could go, she was dead.'

Janet sat in silence, tears started to stream down her face. After some time, she found what she could of her sang-froid, wiped the tears away, and pulled herself upright again, but Blades wondered how long the composure would last.

'That must have been dreadful for you,' Blades said, his voice soft.

'It was. So I know how she must have felt. He was a selfish man. And now I grieve for Miss Evelyn.'

Blades swept his gaze over the three servants as he said with decisiveness, 'You must all let me take your fingerprints, to compare with the others in the room. It'll allow me to eliminate yours.'

They complied. Then, as he had nothing more to ask them for the present, he dismissed them, saying that Peacock would see them later to take their statements. It was time to examine that murder scene further.

# CHAPTER FOUR

'That desk isn't just open,' Peacock said when Blades entered the room. 'It's been forced.'

'Has it now?' Blades strode to the escritoire and studied it, still without touching anything. 'Have you started on fingerprints?'

'I was about to.'

Peacock opened his black leather bag and took out boxes of French chalk and of lampblack, then started on the desk with white powder. It was covered in prints and prints on prints. Most were blurred but a few showed clear loops and whorls. 'Miss Wright's must be all over it,' Peacock muttered.

'And someone else's?' Blades asked.

'Someone else with gloves on,' Peacock replied.

'I see what you mean,' Blades said, studying them. 'Try the poker.'

Peacock brushed chalk on, then took out metal pincers from his bag before turning the poker and trying the other side. When he had finished, Blades took the pincers from him and also studied the poker. Just beside the bloodstain, just there, was a hair. Taking tweezers from his pocket,

Blades picked up the hair to examine it against the light before putting it in an envelope.

'A hair of Miss Wright's?'

'I would think so,' Blades said. 'And the poker was the murder weapon.'

'Looks like it. Good prints on it too.'

'Try the glasses.'

There were clear prints on both of them.

'Good. We can establish if the poker was wielded by her visitor or not,' Blades replied.

'When do you think he put the gloves on?' Peacock asked.

'After she was dead, and he wanted to rifle for the papers he wanted?'

'Why didn't he wipe the prints on the poker?'

'A good question.' Blades sighed, and a frown appeared on his forehead, which slowly deepened.

Peacock continued dusting to Blades' instructions. Once he'd dusted everywhere, Peacock then proceeded to photograph all the prints.

As he did so, Blades busied himself. He had brought his bag with him from which he produced a powerful flashlight. With this, he swept the room, examining every inch of the rug round the body, to begin with, then outward to cover all the carpet, flooring, chairs and other furniture, finishing back where he started, where he began a study of the fireplace. When he was finished, he said, 'The only traces of blood are centred round the body, which suggests the body hasn't been dragged around and that the murder happened where she fell, which fits in with what we thought, a quarrel followed by a couple of quick blows. And, so far, it points to Digby Russell.' Blades continued, 'He was the person last with her, to our knowledge. Janet opened the door to him, though she did not see him leave, and the body was found the next morning by the maid.'

'Unless it was someone in the house,' Peacock suggested.

'Or someone else entered it unseen. The prints might tell us about that.'

'What do we know about Digby Russell?'

'Younger than Evelyn. Much. And he spent a lot of time in her company; providing spiritual support, we're told. She was left on her own by her father's death and presumably came into money, so there could have been other reasons. After all, her father defended her from any young man who ever showed an interest in her. At last, she had the freedom to have a relationship with one, and there was Digby Russell. She must have felt drawn to him.'

'That sounds likely,' agreed Peacock.

'I wonder if he's a man for the ladies among his flock.' Blades was in full flow now and started to speak more quickly. 'But if he had designs on her, why kill her? Did he move too fast on her and alarm her? Did he assault her? Or had she changed her will in his favour? Or was there insurance?'

'Is that likely if they haven't passed the stage of courting, or got to it properly yet?'

Blades nodded. 'If we knew how well that had developed, it would help. Or might there have been something valuable in the desk?' Blades continued to give that thought. 'If it was something in particular the killer wanted, he must have known it was likely to be there, so it was someone who knew her.'

'Or just a quarrel?'

'About what?' Blades paused as he thought about this. 'Though I don't suppose that would matter with someone volatile if something arose. How volatile is Russell? A minister? You wouldn't think he'd fit the bill. Still, as he was there, he's the first suspect.'

Blades liked working with Peacock. He was a good person to bounce ideas off. Battle-hard and battle-bright were the phrases that came to mind when Blades thought

25

of his sergeant. Peacock had also been a sergeant in the army during the war. A self-contained man, he never spoke of it, but Blades knew well enough from others the horrors he must have seen.

Police officers were not conscripted, though they were encouraged to volunteer. Blades had felt he ought to do his bit, but Jean insisted he stay at home. She had lost her brother Tom at the Battle of the Somme and she did not want to lose her husband, so he had continued with his police work. Jean praised him to the skies for it, told him he was being equally useful as a policeman, as someone had to make sure people left at home were safe, but it rubbed at his conscience. While men like Peacock were at war, men like Blades, with less competition to face, gained promotion at home. Perhaps it was the guilt he felt, but, when he looked at Peacock, he had a sneaking suspicion Peacock might be more able than he was, and Blades often felt the need to prove something to him. He could not help remembering the man had won the Military Medal.

Blades sometimes wondered if Peacock resented him, though he did not appear to. Perhaps Blades just thought Peacock ought to. His sergeant was a resilient, spry sort of fellow who got on with his job with apparent stoicism and admirable competence. Blades watched Peacock as he busied himself with the camera. Peacock was a lean man with an unimposing manner, but he was not someone to be underestimated. Those photographs would be clear and comprehensive. The fingerprints would give all the information possible.

# CHAPTER FIVE

Janet opened the door and ushered in Dr Parker, a thin man in his early thirties who looked out of breath and inconvenienced, then horrified when he saw the body.

'Miss Wright,' he said. 'Oh no.' His eyes seemed to goggle as he studied her.

Blades looked at him with interest.

'You knew her?'

'No. And yes. I met her on social occasions around Birtleby, charity dinners and the like. I wouldn't say I knew her personally, but it's dreadful to see her like this.'

He put his bag down beside her. 'Have all the photographs been taken? I can move her to examine her?'

'Yes,' Blades replied.

Parker knelt down, put his hand out to push some hair back from the forehead, and took out a glass to examine her with. He muttered as he wrote down notes in his black notebook. 'How did it come to this?'

Blades found this unusual. When he had worked with Parker before, he had made a display of his objectivity.

After spending time studying the body, Parker said, 'The cause of death seems clear. Killed instantaneously by a blow to the head followed by another one to make sure.

It was unnecessary, but the killer wasn't to know that. The skull is fractured in two places by some blunt instrument. The signs are it was the same one used to make each blow. Death by blunt-force trauma will be the phrase in the report, though we'll check to see if there are indications of anything else in the post-mortem. The first blow probably killed her – by something heavy and presumably handy.' His eyes swept round. 'That poker would have done it, or anything of the same size or weight.' He looked again at the poker. 'There is blood on it. It can be checked to see if it's mammalian.'

'Perpetrated by a man or a woman?' Blades asked.

'A man easily – or a strong woman. The clothing hasn't been disturbed so outrage is unlikely, but we'll cover that in the post-mortem too. I suppose you want an estimate of the time of death?'

'Yes.'

Parker manipulated Miss Wright's hand and arm.

'Stiff. Rigor mortis has set in.' He touched the skin again and considered. 'Absolutely cold. Dead over twelve hours. No more than thirty-six. And it'll probably be impossible to be more accurate than that.'

'Sometime yesterday evening?'

'It would be possible. And I'd better take the internal temperature to check.'

After he had done that, he turned to Blades and said, 'Everybody was hoping she'd get some life to herself after her father died. He was bed-bound for so long, she can't have had much of a time of it. This is tragic.'

'Did you treat him?'

'No, but all this was common knowledge around here. Then she became a bit of a recluse, though she was into séances.' He sighed, tutted, glanced down at her again, then put his instruments into the bag and closed it. He turned, ready to go. 'I'll arrange for an ambulance to take her to the morgue.'

But Blades was still interested in what Parker could tell him. 'Did you hear anything else about her?'

'A sheltered woman, a bit too sheltered. Mid-forties. Past her prime. A shame to get your freedom at last at that stage. Too late for children and a more normal life. The gossip was her father clung onto her and didn't allow her any life.'

'She was a recluse?' Blades asked.

'Yes.'

'That could cut down the suspects,' Peacock said.

'Do you know anything about her friends?' Blades asked Parker.

'The Spiritualist church had its claws into her.'

'Its claws?'

'She was left a wealthy woman by her father, by all accounts. And she was hit by grief, and basically alone. Though there was a brother, I don't think they got on.'

'Digby Russell was her minister. Have you heard anything about him?'

'Sorry. The Spiritualist church isn't my scene. It's not scientific.'

Blades wasn't sure if he was pleased to be reaching early conclusions or not, but Digby was such an obvious suspect: the last known person to have seen Miss Wright alive –a lonely, vulnerable, grieving but wealthy spinster – and him a man fifteen years younger than her who was spending more time with her than people expected of a minister.

'Completely different from our last murder case at least,' Parker said.

'Is it?' Blades replied.

'Those bodies on the shore. He hasn't come back.'

'There are similarities. Death by a blow or blows.'

'But definitely not the same instrument or instruments.'

'No. Were there just different things to hand?'

'Possibly. But I'm only trained to provide medical evidence. You're the detective.'

'Nowhere near a beach at least,' Blades said.

'And a completely different type of victim,' Peacock added. 'It's alright, sir. It's not him. He's not returned.'

'It's my belief he left some time ago, or died,' Dr Parker said. 'Dead probably. We've been discussing that, we doctors. It's a pity no one had the chance to study him, but from the pathology we did see, we don't see why else he would have stopped.'

Blades was embarrassed at his colleagues being so aware of his vulnerability over that case and did his best to keep a placid expression on his face. Three young women found dead on Birtleby beach on his watch, and they still did not know who it was. That left difficult scars. 'There's been nothing in the Police Gazette about similar murders elsewhere,' he said.

'He's dead,' Peacock said.

'Maybe somebody got him,' Blades said, 'none of which helps us with this victim.'

Yet he did need to catch this murderer to help ease the continuing pain from those crimes, although Blades would not put this into words.

# CHAPTER SIX

The centre garden at Elmwood Hall was laid out in a geometric pattern of box hedges round flower beds with, further off, a pond with clear, still water and lily pads, and a summer house overlooking a lawn. It was all neatly kept. The figure of a broad-boned man of middle age was stooped over in a bed of lupins. Trowel in hand, he was pulling at weeds and transferring them to a basket. His skin looked weathered, his expression disgruntled, but his concentration fierce, and he did not look to Blades like someone he would have chosen to disturb. When he and Peacock stood beside him, the figure looked up, glared, looked as if he were about to let loose invective, then paused for thought as he started to take them in, when his expression became questioning instead.

'Mr Falconer? Charlie Falconer?' Blades asked.

'Dead to rights,' Charlie replied as he set down his trowel and stood up. He was not as tall as either Blades or Peacock, but he was strongly built and there was something intimidating in his look. 'You'll be the police inspector?' Charlie said.

'Inspector Blades, and this is Sergeant Peacock. We'd like to ask you some questions.'

'About Miss Wright? It was a dreadful thing that. You wonder what kind of person would do it. I hope you find him quickly.' The tone was a contrast to Blades' first impression of him.

'We try to progress. I don't suppose you saw or heard anything last night?'

'Last night? I was at home in my cottage. My wife Margaret can vouch for that. So I can't tell you what was happening at the house, but if I'd heard anything, I'd have gone out to see what was going on. Miss Wright was a fine lady.'

'About what time did you finish work?'

'About half five and went straight home.'

'And you spent all evening in your cottage after that, just the two of you?'

'I've told you that. Yes.'

'And you weren't aware of anyone visiting the house?'

'I didn't see or hear anything.'

Blades had been studying Falconer as he spoke. Was there something hidden in that now controlled expression? Blades swept his eyes round the garden.

'You're conscientious about your work,' he said.

'I did wonder whether to do my gardening today or not. Miss Wright won't be paying me, but I expect her brother'll see me right.'

'Have you been here long?'

'About a year. The last man was finding it too much for him as he was starting to get on a bit.'

'Has it been a good place to work?'

'I manage the garden fine. Her ladyship was pernickety about her grounds, and she and Janet always wanted more out of that kitchen garden than you could get. But the pay's been regular, and the cottage is fine.'

'So you've mixed feelings about Miss Wright's death?'

Charlie thought for a moment, then flashed a glare at Blades. 'I wouldn't say that,' he said. 'Miss Wright was a fine woman, formal like the rest of her class with servants, but she had a gracious enough manner to her. She just expected you to do your work well and know your place. She treated you with respect, so you always did your best by her. In any case, she made allowances. Margaret suffers dreadfully from arthritis – she's my wife – and Miss Wright realised I needed to spend time with her. She knew that before I came but was happy with it. She was doing a good deed by employing someone in my situation and it was something she liked to do. She was a good woman. But she was demanding about the work. I wondered how I was supposed to manage it sometimes.'

'Was your wife in the big house at all?'

'No. She doesn't go out of the cottage much. She seats herself in the garden now and again, but that's about it.'

'How did the other staff get on with Miss Wright?'

'They just got on with their jobs. I don't know of any ill feeling about anything.'

'Do you know anything about her visitors?'

'I never met them. I work in the garden.'

'Still, it's surprising what servants hear.'

'Her brother visited sometimes. Apart from that, she didn't have much in the way of visitors. I don't think you're supposed to feel sorry for employers – they're your betters, aren't they? – but she was a bit too much on her own after her father died, so you had to. That Digby Russell came around. I didn't think much of that. A young man that age fussing over a woman like Miss Wright. It was plain as the nose on your face what he was after, but Miss Wright seemed to think the sun shone out of him. She thought he put her in touch with her father – so I heard. A load of baloney to get money, if he managed to get any – and I hope not.'

'He was round last night, wasn't he?'

'So Janet said.'

'You're sure you didn't catch any sight of him arriving or leaving?'

'I'm sure.'

'Do you know anything about her relations with her brother?'

'They weren't close, but as everything I know came from Janet and Mary, you'd be better getting it from them. I hope you catch the man who did this, but I doubt there's anything I know that can help.'

There was a finality in the way he said this, and Blades thought it might be true, but he did wonder if Charlie Falconer had been as open as he had pretended. Blades supposed that his initial impression of the man lingered.

'I'll need to take your fingerprints,' he said.

The fierce look returned to Charlie's face. 'Why?'

'Just for elimination.'

'I've never been in the house. I've had to take up vegetables and flowers, but they won't let the gardener past the kitchen.'

'Still, if you don't mind.'

'I suppose.' Then he paused. 'Look, I hope you don't suspect me. I liked Miss Wright. Who wouldn't? She was a kindly soul. It was good of her to give me the opportunity of this job here. Lots wouldn't.'

'I see.' And Blades did see. His understanding of Miss Evelyn Wright was growing. She could be seen as someone to take advantage of.

# CHAPTER SEVEN

It was a solid, stone-built Victorian terraced townhouse, one which did not immediately suggest a penniless adventurer to Blades, and Blades wondered where the money for it came from. The Spiritualist church was not a rich one, to his knowledge. The black, painted door under the glass window with the number 42 in gilt was opened by a sturdy, middle-aged man with a bald pate that shimmered under the light from the street lamp. Blades noticed his fit appearance, and the suggestion of the formidable in the questioning look he gave them.

'Can I help you?' he asked.

Although the man lacked the traditional air of subservience, Blades assumed someone answering the door to a household of this type was a manservant. Blades held out his card and asked to see Mr Russell.

The man took the card and studied it. 'If you'll come this way,' he said.

Blades and Peacock followed him. Blades was about to interview his main suspect and noticed the tension in himself. Blades knew he had to be at his most alert to make certain he missed nothing.

He found himself in a sitting room with gilt-framed pictures and a large, brass gasolier below an ornate plaster centre-piece in the ceiling. The furniture was dark with some handsome, carved pieces. Blades and Peacock found themselves seated in high-backed chairs designed for elegance, not comfort, while the manservant disappeared into the passage.

A tall, thin young man with black, neatly combed hair, and what looked a very deliberate smile, appeared. He offered his hand to each in turn and introduced himself as Digby Russell before seating himself facing them.

'How can I help you, gentlemen?'

Blades allowed a pause as he studied Russell, before replying. Despite the practised smoothness in Digby's manner, there had been a momentary nervous tic under his left eye.

'Have you heard about the death of Miss Evelyn Wright? She came to your church, didn't she?'

'Sadly, yes. It's tragic.'

'Did you know her well, sir?'

'I assisted her through her grief. I thought she was managing to reconcile herself, and I admired her courage. But it must have been hard. Her father suffered a long illness with difficult times.'

Such a formal description of the relationship, Blades thought, and wondered at it.

'Do you know if she had other visitors?'

'To my knowledge, her brother. Do you suspect murder?'

'Why do you ask?'

'You're a police inspector investigating a death. It sounds possible.'

'As you say, it could be.'

It definitely was, and Digby could know that as well as Blades did, but there was no point in spelling things out. Then there was a pause as Digby seemed to digest this.

'She was on various charitable committees, I understand,' Blades continued. 'Was there no acquaintance from them who might be in the habit of visiting?'

'I suppose there might have been, though I don't know of anyone who did. It was some time since she'd been anywhere near any of her charities. As I said, her father had to endure a long illness.'

'When did you last visit Miss Wright?'

While Digby paused before his reply, Blades studied him with care, as, he noticed, did Peacock.

'As you'll know from Janet, I visited last night but didn't stay long. There was something bothering her, and she didn't seem in the mood for conversation with me, so I left.'

'You don't know what might have been upsetting her?'

'Something to do with her brother, I think.'

'You think?'

'She said he had been telling her she ought to sell the house and get somewhere smaller, more suitable for a spinster, and she wondered how he could know if she intended to be a spinster or not.'

'And what did you say to that?'

'I didn't know what to make of it. I felt a bit uncomfortable though because there had been other remarks at different times and I wasn't sure where she was going with them. Ours was a spiritual relationship, not a personal one.'

So Digby was saying he considered Miss Wright had been making a pass at him, or was about to. That was interesting, Blades thought. He had assumed things would be the other way around.

'So you left?'

'Women can become attached to a minister at difficult times. It's not a good idea to take advantage of your position. They're not seeing you as yourself and, being the minister, you can come across as better than you are. It can lead to an unbalanced relationship which wouldn't be desirable.'

Blades wondered if Digby had swallowed a manual on correct ministerial behaviour, and noticed he had been looking slightly past him when saying all that, as if he did not want to meet his eyes. Now Digby looked him straight in the face and flashed what Blades took was his most convincing smile, something which Blades didn't find believable.

'I want to know more about your meeting with Miss Wright. What happened after Janet showed you up?'

'She didn't. She left me to find my own way upstairs. Miss Wright was seated with a book in her hand when I entered. She offered me a glass of port and we chatted. That was about it. I left after about half an hour.'

'So you arrived about when, and left at what time?'

'I must have arrived about seven and left about half an hour later.'

'Where were you standing?'

'I was in front of the fireplace. I left my glass on the mantlepiece and left.'

'You quarrelled, and you left?'

'I wouldn't say it was a quarrel. I was wary of the way the relationship could develop, but I did care for Miss Wright professionally. I chatted about this and that, made excuses of other commitments and left.'

'You didn't argue about anything else?'

'Certainly not.'

Blades noticed the tenseness round Digby's mouth. 'You didn't see anyone else around?'

'No.'

Blades was not convinced by much of what Digby had said but thought it would be a mistake to attempt to pressure him yet and that perhaps he ought to leave things there. Digby had admitted to being there, which was useful, but not to a disagreement. There was circumstantial supposition but no proof of anything, though that could turn up. But there was one question he should ask.

'Do you know anything about Miss Wright's will?'

Digby gave him a wary look. 'When I think about it, she had talked of including a donation to the Spiritualist church, but it wouldn't have been significant, and I don't even know if she did it. I certainly wouldn't kill her for that.'

Blades kept his face neutral. 'As you say, sir. And you wouldn't object if I took your fingerprints for elimination purposes?'

Digby gave him an icy smile, but Peacock soon had Digby's prints neatly placed on card.

# CHAPTER EIGHT

Blades thought it time he and Peacock went back to the drawing room and gave the desk a search. If the quarrel between Digby and Evelyn Wright had been so deep it had led to murder, what might have been the cause?

Blades pulled out the chair and sat in front of the escritoire, lifted the lid and, at first, simply looked. He noted that papers were neatly piled with no signs of a hurried search. Then he started to go through them. He commented to Peacock on what he found. 'Paid bills. Ordered by date of submission of bill. Grocer. Butcher. Gas firm. Dressmaker. Hotel?' Blades paused and leafed through those. 'Unpaid bills in this pile. The grocer. And then there are these: more bills from dressmakers.' He paused, leafed through the piles again and extracted bills. He placed both unpaid and paid dressmakers' bills in one pile before leafing through those. 'She's been spending a lot on clothes lately. What could that tell us?'

'She'd started to dress to impress her young man?'

'Digby?'

'Yes.'

'These are more fashionable than the ones she was wearing that evening, a shorter length of dress for one thing.'

'Perhaps she hadn't got around to wearing them yet?'

Blades was doubtful. 'Her young man is Digby, he's come over for a visit, and she hasn't summoned up the nerve to put her new glad rags on? It might make sense at a stretch, though. As Miss Wright was used to being ultra-respectable, it could have been difficult to change her dress habits at her age. It's one thing to have the dresses, it's another to wear them. What Janet told us does suggest Evelyn was repressed. All the same, does it really sound like a woman to you? When my wife gets new clothes, she likes to show them off.'

Peacock half-smiled as he replied, 'That is what Miss Wright seems to have been like.'

'There was something contradictory about her,' Blades said. 'She had a reputation of being a recluse after the death of her father – in Birtleby – but she travels to a fashionable hotel in Leeds and who knows what she did there? Even the body held contradictory elements if you compared the traditional length of the dress to the short cut of the hair.'

'Her hair was odd,' Peacock said.

Blades frowned. He leafed through more papers.

'Birth certificate for herself, death certificate for her father. Bank statements.'

He leafed through the statements.

'She did have a healthy balance. Her dressmakers' bills hardly dented it. And here's what went out to the grocer, the butcher, the coal company, the gas company, and her hotel.' Blades paused, then leafed through the statements again. 'She'd become fond of staying in that hotel. The Princess Grand in Leeds. She stayed there for weeks at a time and more than once. What were the trips to Leeds about? Did she go with Digby?'

'That might have been when she wore her new finery?'

'I thought she must have worn it somewhere. And Digby joined her there?'

'That would contradict his statement.'

'Wouldn't it? We'll follow that up.' Blades put the bills to one side then lifted up an August document.

'Her will, sealed with wax but the seal broken. Whoever searched the desk read it.'

'After her death? What was he checking on?'

Blades unfolded the will and read it. 'She's left the house to her brother, and twenty thousand pounds. That's motivation for him. And five hundred pounds to the Spiritual Church, which Digby Russell might have access to. People have been murdered for less, though he might have been disappointed if he's our killer. So, we have him at the scene and we have motivation. And five hundred pounds left to Janet. Which could even give her reason to murder her mistress. Now there's a suspect I hadn't considered. I wonder if she knew she'd been left anything?'

'When was the will dated?' Peacock asked.

'A month ago. So it's not been changed long, though possibly Miss Wright did tell one of her beneficiaries the terms of it. And whoever did search the desk, read it and put it back.'

'Thought that's OK and murdered her for it?'

'Or read it after killing her.'

'Callous bastard whichever it was. Is there anything else interesting in the desk?'

Blades probed a bit. 'No,' he said. 'But we can follow up all of this.'

# CHAPTER NINE

There was no point to having the usual grocery order sent without Miss Wright in the house, so Janet went to the grocer's shop to change it. She walked into the centre of Birtleby and over to a good-sized store with a striped awning and a sign above it that took up about a quarter of the frontage: "Cavendish –Grocers to the Nobility". That boast had always impressed Janet as she knew it had some truth in it, not that the nobility made up the bulk of Mr Cavendish's customers, but only the better off did shop here with most people frequenting the weekly outdoor market in the Lawnmarket.

Outside it were displayed crates and barrels filled with fruit and vegetables, the multitude of berries lending an appealing brightness and colour. Once inside, customers were faced with counters on either side, one glass-fronted and displaying meats, the other with brightly labelled tins stacked on top of each other in precarious glory and, at the counter-front, glass-fronted drawers with spices, flour, oats, and various other loose items. Straight ahead was another counter, this one with large scales and an enormous cheddar cheese with a cheese slice beside it, and in front of it lay open barrels with barley and rice and various other offerings. Behind every counter were rows of shelves filled with tins and packets. Behind the centre counter stood a thin, stooped man in brown overalls with what hair he had left swept across his pate in a futile attempt to hide the bareness. This was Mr Cavendish who, at the sight of Janet, flashed his obsequious smile at her. The Wright household order was held in high regard, which is why an anxious look swept across his face when he heard her opening remark.

'Not the regular order?' he replied.

Janet paused as she had no idea how to say what followed.

'We won't be catering for Miss Wright anymore.'

'We won't?'

Janet was embarrassed at the length of her next pause but how could she find the words to say this? Then she decided the simplest way was best. 'Miss Wright was found dead today,' she said.

Cavendish's face showed his shock and there was sincerity in his reply. 'I'm sorry to hear that. Miss Wright? How dreadful.'

'It was Mary that found her,' Janet went on, 'and her just a girl and not long in the household. It was dreadful for her. She'd just gone in to do the fire and I heard her shriek and I thought – I don't know what – maybe someone had come into the house. She wasn't being attacked by someone, was she? Though I don't even know if I had thought it out as well as that. I'd never heard Mary scream like that. She goes about her work so quietly you wouldn't know she was there. I didn't even know she had such a bellow in her. So I rushed in to see what was what and there she was, lying there.'

'Mary?'

Janet bit back an irritated response though she supposed, when she thought about it, that what she had said might have been muddled. She replied, 'Miss Wright.'

Then she paused again to gather her thoughts. 'Covered in blood with a poker lying beside her.'

'No. You can't mean that!'

'I suppose that was what they hit her with.'

'They? Were there a few of them?'

Janet did not try to hide the irritation this time. 'How would I know? They were long gone before Mary found Miss Wright. I don't know what I'm going to tell her mother.'

'God. Poor Miss Wright.'

'She was a proper lady and there she was, lying on a floor with her favourite georgette dress covered in blood. I don't know. The whole world seems turned upside down or come to a stop or something, and what do I do next? Change the grocery order I suppose, though just that seems – I don't know.'

'It's practical. You have to do the practical things. That's how you get through these events. There's no point in brooding, not that I've dealt with a murder but, you know, when my mother died—'

'I know.'

Janet found herself staring at thin air again and lost for words. Then she said, 'They'll have told her brother by now I expect. And we'll all be looking for other positions I suppose.'

'Her brother won't keep you on?'

'Who knows? I don't. Maybe not. Though it's a grand enough house. He might keep it on. Even if he does, it'll all be different. I suppose we carry on as usual till we find out. But the grocery bill won't be the same, and Miss Wright won't be paying for it.'

'We'll present the bill to the estate. Don't worry about that. Who did you say was the solicitor handling it?'

'The family one, as far as I know, Menzies and Carroll. They'll sort it out.'

'Have the police been?'

'They've been all over the place, searching and taking photographs and fingerprints from everybody too, though what any of it has told them so far, I don't know.'

'They haven't any suspects?'

'They haven't told us anything, just asked a lot of questions. I think we're all suspects, as if any of us would do such a thing. Where will we get a roof over our heads next?'

'You'll find a place. Everyone respects you, Janet.'

'We'll see. Anyway, here's the changed order,' Janet said, handing it over. 'I'm sorry it's such a short list. It's just the servants that need to be fed, though I expect we'll have to cater for her brother as well if he decides to come to stay.'

After Janet left, Cavendish passed her news on to his next customer, who in turn told the drama to the next person she met, as did she. Thus the news buzzed around Birtleby.

# CHAPTER TEN

Katy was preparing vegetables in the kitchen when Janet returned. Katy had made sure she was obviously busy for the return of the cook she worked under. Janet's temper would be uncertain at the moment and Katy knew from experience anything she was doing would be fair game for Janet to pick at. And here Janet was, stomping in and putting her bag down with a thud as she took off her coat and hat and hung them on coat hooks. She walked to the kitchen table and studied Katy's carrots.

'We need half of those,' she said.

'Sorry,' Katy said. 'I did the usual. I thought it was what you wanted.'

'Who do we have to cater for now?' Janet asked. 'And we'd better not eat too much if we want to be kept on.'

Katy bit back her reply, though she wondered why there were no new instructions from Janet if she wanted something different.

'There's such a thing as common sense,' Janet continued. 'Go and fetch Mary.'

Katy did and Mary duly trooped back with her. They seated themselves at the table opposite where Janet now sat, obviously marshalling her thoughts, not that Mary gave her time to do much of that with her mind so full of questions.

'Do you know if the police have any idea who did it?' she asked Janet.

'They've told me as much as they've told you,' Janet said, 'which is what you would expect – nothing.'

'Was it Digby?' Mary asked.

'It must have been,' Katy said. 'Who else could it have been?'

'Do you think he'll be back to do any of us in?' Mary asked.

'Why would he do that?' Janet said.

'Why would he do Miss Wright in?' The genuineness of Mary's anxiety was obvious as she sat there wringing her hands.

'For God's sake, girl,' Janet said, then appeared to force a more patient look on her face. 'You're perfectly safe. Stop worrying. I doubt Digby Russell has even noticed you.'

'A friend of mine went to one of his séances,' Katy said. 'She says he's cracked. He puts on this funny voice and acts as if he's a soldier returned from the dead while he gives out messages that are supposed to be from the other side, but he just looks loony, and if he believes that he must be.'

'You don't believe?' Mary said. 'I do. My uncle died at Ypres. That Digby's passed on more than one message from him to my mum. And he mentions things that only my uncle would have known about. It is my uncle.'

'Digby's cracked,' Katy said. 'You can tell that when he comes around here. Look at that nervous tic of his. Some of the soldiers who came back aren't anything like the men they were before. Nancy in the fishmongers told me about her husband. Screaming in the night. About God knows what, and he won't stop. And he never used to lay a hand on her. Now she's got to watch out for his fist whenever he's in a foul mood, which is half the time. And he can't control it, lashes out then realises what he's done afterwards. I could believe that of Digby.'

Mary and Janet watched her with serious expressions.

'If it's Digby, they'll catch him,' Janet said. 'They know about him being round here with Miss Wright all the time. They'll question him.'

'Is that front door locked?' Mary asked. 'He could come marching straight in here.'

'You're right,' Janet said. 'Every door needs to be kept locked all the time now. Katy, go and make sure of them.'

Katy disappeared to check the front and back doors, and the servants' entrance. When she came back, she had a satisfied smile on her face. 'There you are, Mary. All safe. Digby won't be back to batter you to death and spread your blood and guts all over the floor today.'

'Shut up,' Mary said.

'Nor will the postman or the grocer's boy or the milkman. But maybe I will.' Then she laughed.

'It's all right for you,' Mary said. 'You didn't find the body. I got ever such a shock when I saw Miss Wright lying there. I was just doing the cleaning. You don't expect to find a dead body, and not Miss Wright's. I don't know what my mother'll say when she finds out.'

'To business in hand,' Janet cut in. 'We're still employed – by Miss Wright's estate – until told otherwise, and we continue with normal tasks. The difference is we don't need to make meals for Miss Wright, but there's still the house to be looked after and, if we want to be kept on by her brother, we need to make sure it's as clean and neat as a new pin. That front step should have been done better this morning, Mary. And Katy, try to look a bit smarter. Straighten up that cap.'

'Yes, ma'am,' Katy replied, though she resented the tone in Janet's voice. Then a thought occurred to her. 'If it wasn't Digby, who could it have been? Do you think someone could have come in from outside?'

'They must have done,' Mary said. 'It wasn't any of us.'

Katy saw Janet's thoughtful look and supposed her face looked much the same. Then Janet stood up in a brisk movement. 'I'm going downstairs to the office to check the housekeeping books. They need to be up to date. You two get cracking on with the rest of your day's work.' Janet strode out without a backward glance, leaving Mary and Katy looking at each other and pulling faces at her behind her back.

'My mum'll want me home when she finds out,' Mary said.

'You don't want to let her turn you into a scaredy-cat,' Katy said with a scowl. 'Mine wouldn't try to persuade me to chuck in a good job because of this.' Katy, who was an orphan, had never admitted this to Mary and was making this up. One reason she was not leaving at a hundred miles an hour was that she had nowhere else to go.

'I don't understand you,' Mary said.

To which Katy affected a devil-may-care attitude. 'Weren't you glad to get away from home?'

'Yes. But anybody would be scared out of their wits by murder.'

'Wild horses wouldn't drag me away from here.'

'The job's not that great,' Mary replied. 'Do you not hate Janet?'

'Why?'

'She's so strict. She had me dust a room three times in a row yesterday because she wasn't satisfied.'

'Don't worry about that.'

'She picks on me.'

'It's good for you. Don't you know that?'

'I cry myself to sleep some nights.'

'Don't be soft. It's how they go on in the best houses. It gets you up to scratch. You'll see. When you leave here and work somewhere else, you'll find it's a doddle. There's no way I would leave this place. Now I'm in the kitchen, I'm learning to be a cook. Janet's teaching me and she's an expert at it. And I get to watch her all the time. She even lets me do sauces. She says I've got a talent. Once I've been with her a couple of years she's going to see if she can get me a place with a chef. She knows one. Then I'll really get somewhere in service.'

'So she says.'

'Yes. She does.'

'It's not just a way to get you to work like mad, is it?'

'She means it. There's no way I would want to annoy Janet because I know she can do that for me.'

'I never see it coming when she lays into me. She terrifies me.'

With that, Mary rose from her seat to return to work and, after a moment, Katy did the same.

Katy often felt much the same about Janet but didn't admit it even to herself. This was her life. She came from an orphanage, and this was what it had prepared her for. She felt she suited it exactly, not that she'd swallowed everything they told her. They had said this was the station in life that God had called her to, and that she should pray to God for the strength to carry out her duties and give thanks for the privilege of the opportunity.

As far as Katy was concerned, she had never met God, did not expect to, and did not know why someone she had never met should have any interest in her. She considered it bunkum that she was carrying out God's duties, but she was carrying out her own, and she loved working in a kitchen. She liked the discipline of it, took pride in the cleanliness of the kitchen table, scrubbed by her so regularly and so carefully, the shine of the copper pans, scoured with such purpose by her after every use. She loved the litany of menus. They had a cadence of their own and, in worshipping the exactness of the phrase in the instruction, the weight of the ingredient and the timing of the cooking, Katy did find something that carried to her a notion of God.

She could see a blessing in the lightness of a soufflé and the delicacy in a flavour. She had hated the spitefulness of the other girls in the orphanage, and the uncertainty of the patronage or ill-favour of the matrons who ran it. She was under someone's thumb here, but she could see a way to get to a position where she had charge over something, and she worried about losing this. She was young and could get work elsewhere but would she have the opportunities to learn to run a kitchen like the one here? Then a thought came into her head, and she became aware of the glower there must be on her face. She did her best to dismiss it.

# CHAPTER ELEVEN

'She was bright, Evelyn, always brighter than me. She could have led a mission or a conservatory or something like that because there was so much talent in her, and she did have ambition, but father would never have approved. He didn't think that sort of thing suitable for a young lady of her class.'

The man who was speaking lounged on a chaise longue in front of sweeping, brown, velvet curtains in a large sitting room resplendent with well-polished furniture, deep-piled rugs, and large oil paintings on the walls, one in the style of – was that Whistler? Blades wondered if it was an original. From his knowledge of Andrew Wright's wealthy background, it could be. The man himself was of medium height, thickset, with a prominent belly, and balding. His skin was the paleness of someone whose outdoor interests were limited, and his eyes blinked behind gilt-framed thick lenses.

'I'm very sorry to break such bad news,' Blades had told him earlier on when he thought Andrew might be taking the death of his sister a bit too well, though the excuse could be made that things had not finished sinking in with him yet. Blades had his eyes totally focussed on Andrew Wright as he listened to him.

'The sad thing is Father didn't even let her get married. He was all right with me because I was the son, sent away to school, on to university and, of course, once I reached my majority, he settled money on me and I led my independent life. He was disappointed I wasn't interested in business but made himself tolerate my passion for the arts. I write. I do get novels published, which he said he was proud of, though I suspect the opposite. It might have been different if I'd been a major writer but unfortunately, most people have never heard of me.'

'Fathers expect too much,' Blades said.

'But he was over-protective with Evelyn. She was educated by a governess and, when she came out into society, he saw off any young man who showed interest. After mother's death, he leaned on her. I could see why. He'd depended a lot on mother and he used Evelyn to replace her in so many ways. Then he became an invalid. So Evelyn missed out on things.'

'What did your father die of?'

'Cancer.'

'A painful way to go.'

'And slow. Anyone close suffered from watching him. And now, only one year later, this. Poor Evelyn. She didn't deserve this. You don't know, I suppose, when we can hold the funeral?'

'There'll be a post-mortem, but the body can be released after that.'

Andrew's anxiety over this looked genuine. 'Which will be how long?'

'That's not up to me but I doubt it will be long.'

'So we can arrange the funeral after that?'

'Yes.'

A wistful expression came onto Andrew's face as he considered this. 'Music. We'll make the funeral music wonderful. She loved it. Father did at least arrange piano lessons for her with a renowned pianist. She could have performed in concert halls, but father would have considered it vulgar and there was no need for her to earn money, but perhaps she should have done public performances.' Then a thought seemed to strike him. 'I suppose – whoever killed her didn't interfere with her in any way? She wouldn't have liked that.' There was horror on Andrew's face now, at the thought of this, and Blades replied quickly.

'There was no indication of that.'

'And just the one blow did it?' There was urgency in Andrew's questioning.

'There were two, but the first would have killed her immediately.'

Now Andrew said nothing, just stared back. Then relief expressed itself on his face. 'That's something to be thankful for.' Then the realisation of her death seemed to hit him properly, and he looked away from Blades in a struggle to regain control.

'Did you see much of your sister after your father died?'

Andrew forced himself to look back at Blades. He spoke slowly when he replied. 'I think I expected to see more of her. I checked up on her at first, but she settled down and we got on with our separate lives.'

'When was the last time you saw her?'

Andrew's regret soured his mouth and his voice became halting. 'About a month ago. It was her birthday and I took her out to lunch.'

'How was she?'

'Cheerful. Chatting about that Spiritualist church which I told her to give up on, even if she did maintain that it helped.' Andrew's tone was becoming more even now.

'What did you think of this Mr Digby Russell?' Blades asked him.

'The minister? Never met him but he sounded suspicious to me. I thought the Reverend Watt from the Methodist Church was sound enough.'

'In what way was Digby Russell suspicious?'

Andrew looked thoughtful. He sighed. 'I thought she was too taken with him. I warned her about the type of man who might hang around a single woman with the money she had. She was sheltered.'

'Why might Digby Russell have been a bad idea for her?'

'A few reasons I can think of. He was shell-shocked in the war for one thing, and I've met a few of those. They can be downright creepy. And unpredictable. She felt so sorry for him and he was always round there. He's just helping, she'd say. No minister would be round that much. He was after something. And I would be surprised if he had much money.'

'You say he was shell-shocked?'

'I heard it straight from Evelyn.'

'You didn't try to meet him?'

'My sister was an adult. Our father did too much interfering. I thought it was time she was allowed to lead her own life. But I did ask her about Digby when we met.'

'Did she ever complain about him, talk about arguments or threats? Was there any sign she might have been afraid of him?'

'No. She thought too much of him. That was all.'

'Do you know the terms of your sister's will?'

'I know what she told me. She said she was leaving me the house and all her money.'

'No doubt the solicitor will be in touch.'

'Yes.' Andrew grimaced as if the thought of this was distasteful.

'I'm sorry we have to ask but this is a routine question for all those concerned or related. Would you tell me your movements on the evening of July the 26th?'

Andrew Wright stared back at him. 'Mine? You don't have me down as a suspect, do you?'

'It's a routine question.'

'You don't think I could have done that to Evelyn?'

'I don't, sir, but I have to ask everyone.'

'I suppose.' He glared at Blades as he replied, 'I was at the opera in Harrogate with a lady friend.'

'What time did the performance begin and end?'

'It began at seven-thirty and ended at eleven.'

'Thank you, sir. And the name of the friend?'

Andrew told him and gave Blades her address.

'One more thing, sir. Could I take your fingerprints?'

Andrew looked livid at the suggestion. 'Now that is impertinence.'

'We've taken fingerprints at the scene and if we can eliminate the fingerprints of the innocent then we can isolate the prints of the guilty, which would be useful.'

This did not sound convincing even to Blades. From what he assumed of housekeeping habits at Elmwood Hall, Andrew Wright's prints should not be anywhere near that sitting room, unless he had been there on the night of the murder. Fortunately, Andrew agreed to co-operate.

Blades did spend a moment pondering how long it would take to travel to Harrogate from Birtleby and return, in the motor car parked in Andrew Wright's drive, but thought it would not matter if it was established that he was at the opera at seven-thirty as he had said. Digby had said in his statement that he did not leave Miss Wright till about seven-thirty.

# CHAPTER TWELVE

Blades stood in the conference room at Birtleby Station and looked at the sergeants and constables seated in front of him with their notebooks and pencils poised. It was a pleasant morning and sunshine from the window illuminated the left side of his audience, which made one or two uncomfortable in the glare. Blades asked himself if he was summarising progress for himself or his force. Had he made any? He struggled with self-doubt for an awkward moment then, forcing a confident expression onto his face, proceeded to hold forth in his clearest, most authoritative voice.

'First, the murder scene.' He pointed to a photograph of Evelyn Wright's body that was pinned to the board behind him. 'Found dead at eight o'clock in the morning by the parlour-maid, Mary Cunningham. As you can see, Evelyn Wright was struck with two blows, the first of which would have been enough by itself to kill her, which means he must have wanted to make sure, and both probably came from the poker lying beside her. Fingerprints were taken at the site. A bottle of port lay on one side-table with Miss Wright's fingerprints on it. There were two glasses on the scene, one of which still contained port. This also held Miss Wright's fingerprints. One glass was on the mantlepiece. This one was empty and held the fingerprints of Digby Russell, a Spiritualist minister. Janet the housekeeper has given a statement saying that he visited her that evening. He let himself out and Janet didn't see her mistress again that evening. The next time she was seen was when her body was found the next morning by Mary Cunningham. The police surgeon said she would have been killed sometime that evening, which has been confirmed by the post-mortem, and that was when Digby Russell was there. On the face of it, the minister did it.

'We've interviewed him, and butter wouldn't melt in his mouth, which never means anything. The fact he suffered from shell-shock might be significant. He speaks to the dead, or leads séances anyway.'

One or two of the men sniggered.

'And people believe him. He helps them.'

The sniggers stopped.

'Whether he has a propensity for violence in his background we don't know. He has no police record, but we'll be interviewing his doctor. He ought to know something about Digby's general mental state.'

'If we've got our man, what are we looking for now, sir?' someone asked.

'Yes. Have we got our man?' Blades turned and looked at the photograph of Evelyn, then down at papers on his desk. 'We have the fingerprints of the servants and the family. We're not aware of anyone else who was likely to visit. There are fingerprints in the room of Miss Wright, Digby Russell, Janet the housekeeper, and Mary the parlour-maid. There are no fingerprints belonging to Andrew Wright, the brother. On the desk are the fingerprints of Miss Wright, Mary Cunningham, and some unknown person who wore gloves.'

He paused to allow his men to consider the information they had been given, then continued, 'The desk was opened. Only Miss Evelyn Wright could tell us whether anything is missing. The will was opened and read, probably after Miss Wright's death.'

'Who benefitted?' A different voice, this time from the back of the room. It was Constable Flockhart, always one to ask questions, which Blades liked.

'The brother, Andrew Wright, Janet the housekeeper, and Mr Digby Russell's church.'

'Which could still suggest Digby Russell?' Flockhart continued.

'Apparently.'

'And the motive would be money?'

'The post-mortem shows no indications of sexual assault. Money is a possible motive and Digby Wright might have had reason to think he would benefit financially, he was the last person known to have seen her alive, and he has the strength to inflict those wounds. And the simplest solution is usually the correct one. But…'

'But what?' This was Sergeant Milne, moustachioed and severe.

'There was blood on the poker and it was mammalian. There was also a hair which has been confirmed did belong to Evelyn Wright but…' Blades paused again. 'The fingerprints on the poker were not the fingerprints of Digby Russell, not that they match the fingerprints taken from any other possible suspect but, if we arrest Digby Russell for this, we have to explain that to a jury. Which would be difficult.'

And Blades would have to find a way to explain it to himself. There had been enough trouble in the last case with arresting innocent men and he did not want anything else on his conscience. He was relying on any evidence they had.

'So we dismiss Digby Russell?' This was a voice that came from Blades' right, from a fresh-faced constable whom Blades did not know.

'We'll continue to investigate him and, if we come up with convincing evidence and an explanation of that poker, we can proceed against him. But we can't stop looking elsewhere. The brother is a possibility, if unlikely. There is an alibi which we have to verify. He benefits the most from his sister's will but he is apparently wealthy in his own right, though we will check with his bank to verify his current financial standing. He's a bit of an odd bod. Fifty. Never married. A confirmed bachelor. Why? When he's obviously eligible? This may have nothing to do with anything. In any case, we can only consider him if we can show he could have been at the scene.'

Blades looked down at his desk again. 'I have reports from constables, and I will need more of those. As we haven't placed anyone else in that drawing room, we need to continue questioning neighbours and ask the grocer's delivery men, the postman, bus conductors, anyone who might conceivably have information, to see what strangers have been around. Can we place anyone else anywhere with Evelyn Wright? She'd become a bit of a recluse which should narrow people down, but if it's not Digby we do have to place someone at the scene. We haven't even found anyone else in the locality she'd been mixing with recently. As you carry out your duties in the neighbourhood, ask about. And there might be another witness somewhere. Usually, you do find someone who saw something, and that leads you to something or someone else, and so on. It's a pity no one's seen anything helpful so far in this case. There has been a report in the *Birtleby Times* so someone may come forward with useful information. Meanwhile, those of you on normal duties now know what we're looking for, and the sergeants have organized rotas and areas for others, and they'll communicate those to you.'

Blades referred to notes again. 'Apparently, she'd started travelling around. We have the name of a hotel in Leeds she stayed in, so we will check there. And thank you. Continue with your duties.'

The men put their notebooks and pencils away and muttered amongst themselves as they stood up and proceeded to leave.

# CHAPTER THIRTEEN

When Blades and Peacock were again shown into Digby's ornate sitting room, the first thing Blades noticed was that the butler stayed in the room with them. After motioning them towards chairs, he seated himself beside Digby. Blades gave Digby an inquiring look. 'You want your manservant present during police inquiries?' He wondered just how nervous this suspect was.

'You're under a misunderstanding,' Digby said. 'He's more of a general factotum and friend.'

'Is he?' Blades said, who had never heard of such a thing.

'The relationship goes back a bit,' the 'servant' said as Blades again took in the uprightness of his bearing and the firmness in the voice. 'My name's Eric, Eric Blair. I was a friend of a friend, to begin with. I was visiting someone else in Craiglockhart Hospital when I came across Digby.'

'Go on,' Blades told him.

'That's the hospital where they treated shell-shocked patients.'

'I've heard of it.'

'He was in quite a state.' Eric paused as he gathered his words. 'As were a lot of them. I'll tell you about one. He was shot in the leg and taken to a field hospital where his wound recovered, but his right arm remained useless to him. He couldn't move it. Stiff as a corpse it was. Which was odd because he hadn't been shot there. There was no wound whatsoever. The mind does funny things. Take Digby.'

Blades noticed Digby tensing at this. 'Do you have to?' Digby said.

'The inspector needs to understand.'

'I suppose.'

'He was shell-shocked but the opposite of violent. He was unable to speak or, apparently, hear or move. He didn't anyway. Just sat and stared into space. What he'd seen in the war had so appalled him he'd totally withdrawn into himself. Though mind you, when I came across him, he'd advanced from that. He was talking a bit and moving about, recovering.'

Eric paused, took out a pack of Woodbines and lit one. He drew in from the cigarette, then stared at the smoke as he breathed it out.

'I need to get this right,' he said, 'so that you understand it. When he came out of his silence, he started jabbering quite a bit. Not to anyone at all most of the time, just himself, or so everyone thought. Then they realised he was talking to people, but not to anyone who was actually there. He seemed to be imagining his dead comrades were there beside him. He was talking to them.'

Blades looked at Digby who was sitting very still and quiet as if hating having to listen to this.

'It was a dreadful thing that war,' Blades said. 'It must have been awful out there.'

'You weren't out?' Digby said.

'No,' Blades replied, momentarily feeling the need to defend himself but not finding anything to say.

'It was awful,' Digby said. 'Those machine guns mowing everyone down. Everyone in my platoon was chopped down at the knees as we moved forward at the

Somme. But the bullets missed me completely. Now, why was that?' The look Digby gave Blades as he waited for an answer was accusing. Blades did not know what to reply.

'Some people feel guilty because they're still alive,' Eric said. 'Digby does. So he's glad to be able to help people.'

'So many people dying. So many. How does the mind cope with that?' Digby said. 'It's incomprehensible. Where did they go? They must have gone somewhere. That's what people think. That's why they come to me.'

Blades looked at him carefully. He supposed it would be difficult to doubt that sincerity.

'Anyway, I was saying.' Eric paused again and took in a particularly deep breath of smoke. 'Some of them on the ward started getting séances up. I think most of them were larking around. And they roped Digby into it. They thought it would get him talking a bit with other people, the ones in the room. Not that it happened in the way they intended. Digby became their medium. The dead spoke to his fellow patients through him. Digby wasn't someone who'd be having a bit of fun. They could see that. Then they realised all that time Digby had seemed to be talking to himself, he hadn't been. The dead had come back and were talking to him.'

As Blades watched Eric lean forward in his chair with an intent stare, he could see that the man was serious.

'Were they?'

'You're not a believer?' Eric asked.

'Eric is,' Digby said. 'He always has been. He was a worker in the Spiritualist church for years before he met me.'

'When I found out about Digby, I watched him in his séances and I realised this was someone who could be a big help in our church. He was never passed fit for active service again, but he did recover as such and, when he did, I was in touch with him and welcomed him into our community. In time he became a minister and has been doing countless good for us and for so many grief-stricken families for a couple of years now.'

'I'm glad to hear that. What was the name of the doctor who treated you at Craiglockhart, Mr Russell?'

Digby's eyes widened, and he looked as if he was considering refusing to reply, but he said, 'Dr Anderson. Dr Philip Anderson. There were other doctors, but he was the one who supervised my case.'

'And the name of your doctor here?'

Digby forced the words out. 'Dr Summerfield.'

'Good. Thank you, sir.'

'You're not convinced, are you?' Eric said to Blades.

Blades gave him a casual glance, then looked back at Digby who had shifted in his seat and seemed to be biting his lip. Then, turning to Eric, Blades said, 'It's early in the investigations, sir. We're not convinced about anything.' But what he was thinking was that there was no way Digby was innocent. There must be some explanation for that poker.

# CHAPTER FOURTEEN

Dr Humbold was a middle-aged man; his face was careworn, due to work Blades assumed but, though serious, it was a kind face. Blades was looking at him behind his desk in his consulting room. The doctor's surgery was a converted sitting room in an ordinary house, with a waiting area adjacent, where Blades had noticed several patients seated.

'What can I do to help you, Inspector?'

'I wanted to talk to you about one of your patients.'

'Which one?'

'Digby Russell.'

'That young man? What is it you want to know about him?'

'You'll have heard about the murder of Miss Evelyn Wright?'

'Oh yes. Everyone in Birtleby has heard about that. Is Digby Wright a suspect?'

'Unfortunately, yes, and we know he has a history of shell-shock. What I want to ask is if, in your clinical experience with him, you consider him to be a young man with a propensity to violence.'

'Violence? Digby Russell?' Dr Humbold looked surprised but gave it thought and, as he did, the lines on his forehead deepened. 'I can't, of course, divulge confidential information.'

Blades, who already knew that, waited to see what the next response would be. He hated trying to elicit the help of doctors but, as he was aware how unhelpful any sign of irritation on his part would be, he kept as patient an expression on his face as he could muster.

'But there might be things I could say that would help. It's not my impression Digby is a violent man. He strikes me as being somewhat innocent, not a predator, and somebody who is more likely to be manipulated than to do the opposite.'

'May I ask what makes you say that?'

'A lot of my patients believe in Spiritualism, and he believes in what he's doing. I don't get the impression he's any kind of fraud.'

'Would you say he hallucinates?'

Dr Humbold sat back in his chair and his eyes perused Blades as he sighed. He tapped his fingers. He said nothing.

'You won't answer that question?'

'I can't.'

'I'm sorry if I crossed the line. I didn't mean to.' Though if Blades could have forced a detailed clinical analysis from Dr Humbold, he would have done. 'Thank you, sir,' he said. 'You've been very helpful.'

Then, to Blades' surprise, Dr Humbold volunteered another piece of information.

'He could be influenced by someone else, which might be what is happening with his séances. He's very much under the influence of Eric Blair.'

'Who takes advantage of the form his hallucinations take?' Peacock said.

As a frosty look had come over Dr Humbold, Blades continued, 'The voices that come to him from beyond the grave, shall we say?'

'Though I've no definite knowledge of what I've just said, you understand?' Humbold replied. 'It's speculation.'

'Of course, sir. I do. By any chance, did you have communication with his doctor at Craiglockhart?'

'Yes, and I can't divulge it to you.'

This Blades had expected, though he did wait for a few moments to give Dr Humbold the chance to add anything he wished. As Dr Humbold said nothing, Blades said, 'Have you any idea whether that doctor is still there?'

'You do know that Craiglockhart closed down, don't you? That was only operative for a couple of years.'

'Was it?'

'It was a war hospital. Those doctors will have scattered all over the place by now. Perhaps if you looked up a medical directory, that would tell you where he is.'

'Perhaps. Anyway, you've been more than helpful. Thank you again. I'll leave you to your patients.'

'I'm glad to have been able to help you.'

\* \* \*

When Blades and Peacock returned to their car, Peacock said, 'No doubt you read something into the fact he didn't answer that question about Digby possibly hallucinating?'

'Digby hallucinates. That's what I read into that. And you'd think getting confused about reality would make him dangerous, even if it's not the picture that Humbold wants to paint. Something doesn't add up about that. Humbold says Digby's not a predator, yet his relationship with Evelyn Wright suggests he was out to take advantage of her, which fits in with what other people tell us. On the other hand, he has no history of violence that we know of and he doesn't look violent to me, just weak.'

'Maybe you haven't seen the things I've seen.'

Blades looked inquiringly at him.

'In the war. It's surprising how violent these weak ones can be.'

'Is it?'

'Yes.' But Peacock did not elaborate.

'It's easy to get a gut feeling about Digby, isn't it?' Blades said.

'A pity about the fingerprints on the poker,' Peacock said.

Blades was glad to be reminded of this. 'You're right,' he said, 'Supposition is fine. But proof's what matters. Which won't stop me checking out that hotel in Leeds. I'd love to know if Digby spent time with Evelyn Wright there. If he and Evelyn did shack up there, I would think he's our man.' But even as he said it, doubts emerged in his mind. In that last case, they had been convinced more than once about who committed the murder, only to get it wrong. If Digby was innocent, Blades wouldn't want him to go through what Harry Barker and Bob Nuttall had. The inquest had pointed the finger straight at them because they had looked so guilty, only for facts to prove otherwise later. They must have gone through hell in prison, on remand too. After what they had been through in the trenches, he, the great Inspector Blades, had made them go through that.

# CHAPTER FIFTEEN

The next day came the routine of a brief inquest when due formalities were gone through at which nothing surprising transpired, but, after that, Blades and Peacock were free to go to Evelyn Wright's hotel in Leeds. The Princess Grand Hotel Leeds certainly lived up to its soubriquet of grand, Blades thought as he and Peacock stood outside the three-storey, stone-built edifice fronted by the classical pillars of its front portico. The lawns in front of it deserved to be described as such too.

'How the other half live,' Peacock muttered.

'If this was the hotel Evelyn stayed at, she had good taste.'

'Haven't I heard of this place before?' Peacock asked. 'Didn't Queen Victoria's son Eddie bring one of his mistresses here?'

'I don't know. I don't read the scandal sheets myself. Prince Eddie, eh?'

'And Queen Victoria herself? Wasn't that another woman who was at a loose end after the death of the man in her life? Wasn't there talk about her and that Highland servant of hers, Brown?'

'I did hear about that.'

'It's human nature, isn't it, sir?'

'Which we always seem to meet the worst of. I sometimes wish I could see less of it, but never mind. Here we are, Leeds, the scene of Miss Wright's adventures away from home. What did she get up to outside the goldfish bowl of Birtleby?' There was a weary tone to Blades' voice as he said this, but a briskness in the stride of the two policemen as they walked into the reception area of The Princess Grand.

It was a large space, with a desk on the right-hand side of the entry and elegant, cushioned chairs to the left where a couple was seated in relaxed poses: he, besuited in a fine grey cloth; she, resplendent in her well-cut blue linen day dress. They looked askance at Blades and Peacock, who appeared much as they were, underpaid and over-sombre policemen. Blades strode to the reception desk where a stout man with short-cut black hair and a pencil moustache stood and aimed a polite smile at him. Taking in the man's bearing, Blades assumed him to be the manager.

'Can I help you, sir?'

Blades showed his card. 'I'm here investigating a case.'

'Yes, sir,' the man replied; his professional demeanour slipped as he unconsciously tugged at his sleeve.

'We're trying to establish the movements of a lady called Miss Evelyn Wright, who would have travelled here from Birtleby and stayed about a month or so ago.'

'I'll look at our register, sir,' the manager replied as he drew towards him a large book which lay open on the counter. 'About a month ago, you say?'

'That's when she would have left, probably about the 26th. She would have stayed with you for about a month before that.'

The man turned the pages. 'Here you are. This is when she left.'

'You've found her. At first go. That was efficient.'

'She did sign out on June the 26th. I'll try to see when she signed in.' He turned more pages. 'Here she is. Arrived on May the 20th. Stayed in a room with an adjoining sitting room on the first floor. Is there anything else I can do to help?'

'Do you remember her by sight?'

'I do. A well-mannered lady, softly spoken, expensively dressed. Not overdemanding. An acceptable class of person to have around the hotel.'

Blades wondered at the hesitation the manager made that statement with, and what that might mean. 'Do you know if she met up with anyone while she was here?'

'She did mix with other guests. And she sometimes shared a table with a Mr Osgood, who didn't stay but whom she knew from somewhere else. I remember him. Very careless about where he parked his car. Big, flashy model. A Bentley Sports no less, but he put it anywhere. We were always having to ask him to shift it, so the other guests could get their cars in or out.'

And perhaps that was the reason for the reserve. The company she kept. 'He was definitely called Osgood, not Russell?'

'For sure. Osgood. He was a bit of a loud, unforgettable person.'

Blades and Peacock swapped looks. Perhaps this Osgood explained the uncooperative evidence in Birtleby.

'An arrogant type?'

'Very. Came from a good class though. Posh accent. Careless manner. A generous tipper.'

Blades noticed Peacock looking unprofessionally agog. But it was no wonder. This was a different type of person in the case.

'How did the relationship between him and Miss Wright appear?'

'Casual. Close. They seemed to enjoy each other's company hugely. I assumed there was a romantic relationship, but the waiters might tell you more – or the maids.'

'Did you hear what they spoke about?'

'No. Again, the waiters could have done, though whether they took note of it or not I don't know.' The manager shrugged his shoulders rudely, Blades thought. Perhaps he was tiring of the questions. Then, with a frown on his face, the man asked, 'May ask why you are enquiring after Miss Wright? She seemed a law-abiding lady.'

'I don't doubt it but she's dead. Murdered.'

'God. When did it happen?'

'At her home in Birtleby a couple of days ago. We've been making inquiries in Birtleby and we're spreading our net wider now.'

'There won't be any publicity for this hotel, will there? Customers wouldn't like that.'

Blades gave him a reassuring look. 'In my experience the public love that sort of thing. You'll probably find them flocking to stay in the same room she stayed in. But we'll try to keep you out of the public eye. Don't worry.'

'I would prefer it.'

'I don't suppose you know how I can get in touch with this Mr Osgood?'

'No. But someone else might.'

Then Blades and Peacock found themselves interviewing several members of staff, including a waiter called Joe Perkins. He was a small man approaching middle age who looked a bit careworn. He had an obsequious smile which Blades was suspicious of, but he told himself to beware of prejudice.

'Jack Osgood? Now there's a fellow.'

Blades was pleased to learn his first name.

'Biggest swank you're likely to meet, with his bright silk waistcoats and his gold pocket watch and flashy rings; and he likes a fat cigar after dinner too. Loud voice. You can't miss it from across the room. Charming fellow though. Enormous smile on him and when it comes your way you feel like you're the most important person in the world even if you are only his waiter. Only a young fellow. I did wonder what he could see in that Evelyn Wright. He had plenty of money and could have got anyone. And Evelyn Wright? It was Wright, wasn't it? She loved all the attention he smothered her with. I suppose he made her feel young again. Though you could see she meant nothing to him.'

'Do you know where we can get in touch with him?'

'I don't know his address but he's often at the local dancing hall, the Plaza at St Olaf Square – does a flashy tango, and a slick two-step. Very popular with the ladies. I know because I've seen him there when I've been out with my girl.'

'A proper lady's man?' Blades said.

'You could say so,' Joe Perkins replied. 'Young women like the way he throws money about too.'

Now, what would a man like him want with Evelyn Wright? Blades thought as he decided to visit the Plaza.

Before going on to do that, they talked with the maid who did the rooms on Miss Wright's floor, a plump woman with tired hair and an even wearier expression.

'Miss Wright?' she said. 'A real lady, but they're always the ones who surprise you, aren't they?'

'Are they?' Blades asked.

'She arrived with all her grand airs and posh luggage. All so proper, but after she's been here a few days, there's this new and that new to show off her figure and legs. And then she started wearing lipstick, and the type of scent she used changed. That new Chanel No 5 – and you don't get more expensive than that.'

'You're sure that's Evelyn Wright you're talking about?'

'That was the name. I suppose she started dressing so young because of that bloke she went around with. I think it's sad when a woman does that. I expect he was after her money. She had plenty of it by all accounts.'

'And you know all this how?'

'By the clothes hanging on the rails in her room and what she kept on her dressing table, and by seeing her go about. And she had a man in that room a few times. You could tell by the sheets. Not that I saw who it was. But the talk in the hotel was that it was Jack Osgood she was seeing.'

'Thank you,' Blades said as they took their leave of her.

Blades was surprised by what he'd learned but Peacock looked as if it was only what could have been expected. As they went back to the car, they exchanged thoughts.

'They could put this in one of your scandal sheets, Sergeant.'

'Indeed, sir. So perhaps it wasn't Digby Russell – unless we find more evidence leading to him.'

'At least we wouldn't have to explain why the wrong fingerprints were on the murder weapon – though we'll have to check Osgood's prints too.'

'I'm sure a fishy character like Osgood must have done something, sir, even if it wasn't this.' There was relish in the way Peacock said this, but Blades felt just curious about what they were finding out, if sad.

'But it does sound as if Evelyn was having fun,' Blades said, 'and for the first time in her life, so who can blame her? But perhaps it's not surprising it turned out badly. Poor Miss Wright. She was an innocent abroad. If she didn't have Digby Russell sniffing around for opportunities, she was the one making eyes at him, and when she goes away from home, she has this Jack Osgood at her heels.'

'We're assuming Jack Osgood was a gold digger?'

Then Blades realised what was upsetting him. Elspeth had been a corpse, but she was coming back to life. He did hope he would find this killer.

'He was a real man for the ladies by the sound of it. He could land a much younger and more attractive woman than the dumpy, middle-aged Miss Wright, and yet he made up to her. He doesn't sound the sort of man to be attracted by someone's personality. It had to be her money he was after,' Blades said.

'He's supposed to have money himself.'

'We need to substantiate that. We need to know a lot more about this Jack Osgood, and we need his fingerprints. We need to see if we can place him at the scene. If we can get the constables to show a photograph of him around Birtleby, that might help too.'

'Unless he has an alibi.'

'Which is why the fingerprints will be so important, but, first of all, we need to talk to him, so we'd better go down to that dance hall and see what we can find out.'

# CHAPTER SIXTEEN

It was afternoon, but the Plaza was already in full swing. Blades was impressed by the ambience of the place. The Plaza boasted a lacquered pavilion with lanterns and a faux Chinese village montage. Looking at the couples happily one-step and two-stepping away, the cedar floor was a joy to dance on. The syncopated rhythm of the dance band created an easy mood, and Blades would have been happy to listen to it. The rag that the piano player was bouncing out was cheerful, and the drums, clarinet, and tuba complemented it.

Most of the couples seemed ordinary enough but Blades was not sure about what transactions might be taking place between some of the young gentlemen and dancers, as some of these young ladies were obviously professional dancers at least. Blades thought someone like the man he imagined Jack Osgood to be would be in his element here, flitting in and out between these sylphs and taking his pick. But Blades wasn't here to investigate them, just to find Jack Osgood and question him, or find out some more about him at least.

The manager was a man in his forties with sleeked-back hair, loud braces over a striped shirt, and particularly well shone black patent leather shoes, but, as he was inclined to weight, the cotton shirt was well filled out at the front. When he smiled, the word that suggested itself to Blades was unctuous. Blades showed him his card and he blanched, which made Blades wish he was investigating the dance hall, but he was there on more important matters.

'So how can I help you?' Peter Sloane said, for such was the name the manager had given.

'We're trying to locate a person we are told is a frequent customer of yours.'

'Who are you trying to track down?'

'We have no photograph, but we have a name. We're looking for a young man called Jack Osgood. He's in his twenties. Excellent dancer, I'm told.'

'Jack Osgood?' A serious expression was on Peter Sloane's face now. 'I know the name all right. I'm not sure I wish I did, but he keeps turning up.'

'So, what have you got against him, sir?' Blades asked.

Sloane pulled on a cigarette. 'I've no reason to have anything against him, except he's too cocky and I wouldn't trust him just from looking at him. He'd sell his grandmother. It's written all over him. And did he do it? He has loads of money, too much for a young guy like him, and you can't see what he's doing to earn it.'

'But all you have against him is suspicion.'

'If you like, but if you met him you might agree. He's so self-opinionated and there's something cold there.'

'I'd like to talk to him,' Blades said. 'So where can we find him?'

Despite his eagerness to meet up with Jack Osgood, Blades couldn't help giving the dance hall a lingering look on the way out. Some of these dancers might be up to reprehensible things and, as a policeman, he couldn't avoid noticing that, and suspecting it when he didn't, but that rhythm was catching and, after the war years, who wouldn't be attracted to that mood of gaiety? He could see why Osgood enjoyed spending time there.

# CHAPTER SEVENTEEN

When Blades did find Osgood, he was met with the full force of Jack Osgood's appealing smile and he could see what that waiter Perkins had meant when he described it. Jack Osgood seemed to smile with his whole being and project a warmth and innocence intended to make you feel special and somehow vindicated, though about what wasn't clear. It was wasted on Blades. His response to a superfluity of charm was to check if his wallet had gone missing, but the effect Jack Osgood could have on women was obvious.

As they'd managed to discover Osgood's address from one of the dancers, they'd gone to it, and then found themselves in Jack Osgood's front room. The decoration was in geometric forms in the latest fashion, and a bronze lamp whose base was in the shape of a nubile and naked young lady also caught the eye. There was a large painting over the fireplace which appeared to have been assembled out of cubes. Blades knew enough about fashion to be aware that these were all the trappings of the young and rich. Jack Osgood was seated on a white, wide-winged armchair. He was about five feet ten and slim, and he sat in an easy pose. His hair was a deep chestnut brown and held a wave that gave lightness and grace to his face. He wore the kind of silk waistcoat the waiter had described, and the thick gold chain belonging to the watch in its front pocket flashed. He leaned back, the ankle of one leg leaning on the thigh of the other, his hand carelessly stretched over it. In this pose, the black-and-white patent leather shoes were particularly prominent. The way he sat seemed to be chosen to show he considered himself in control of any situation that might occur. When Blades showed his card to him, Osgood's eyes showed no flicker of reaction, the look on his face remaining lazy.

'Is it a donation to the police benevolent fund you're after? I did make one to the Chief Constable in person only a few weeks ago.'

About the same time as a pink elephant flew past your drawing-room window, Blades thought but did not say. 'We're here on a different matter,' Blades replied.

Osgood raised a cultured eyebrow.

'We've been told you're friends with a lady we have an interest in.'

Osgood allowed a grin. 'I know a few.'

Blades did his best not to let Osgood annoy him, but he suspected he would find it hard. 'Perhaps that's what's led to this situation, sir.'

'Really?' Then Osgood dismissed his surprise and adopted a look of boredom. 'What do you mean by that?'

'You're acquainted with a lady by the name of Evelyn Wright?'

'Evelyn?' His eyes widened slightly.

Osgood's jugular looked inviting and Blades did not beat about the bush. 'She's been found dead, murdered. As you're an acquaintance of hers, it's my duty to ask you for your whereabouts at the time.'

Osgood's smile became cold and his eyes hard. 'And what was the time?' he said.

'The evening of Thursday, 26 July 1921. Can you tell me your movements on that night?'

'That's not long ago,' Osgood said as he considered. 'But, d'you know, I have to think about it. Let's see. Yes. I was at the Plaza Ballroom. That's the dancing club at St Olaf Square.'

'Thank you, sir, and can you tell me what time you arrived and when you left?'

'I would have arrived at, I don't know, about seven and left at about – oh God, when would it have been – about two in the morning. We had a good evening.'

'Your witness would be?'

'Anyone who happened to be in the hall at the time, though I can give specific names.' Then, despite his previous air of vagueness, he gave precise contact details so quickly and easily the answers seemed prepared.

'If this checks out, you seem to be off the hook, sir.'

'Don't sound disappointed, Inspector.' Then Osgood fixed him with a meaningful stare. 'I am upset about Evelyn. I'm sorry. I don't burst into tears. But I did like her.'

'As you say, sir.'

'You will get the bastard who killed her, won't you? I'd like to sort him out myself.'

Blades considered this. He supposed the irate reaction Osgood was displaying now might be genuine, but he thought it unlikely. He suspected the man in front of him didn't have that much depth of feeling. But he just replied to what Osgood had said. 'You might, but I wouldn't advise it, sir.'

'That's a pity.'

'Did you see her a lot when she was staying at The Princess Grand?'

'Now and again. We were friends. I'm in need of a mother. My own's dead and Evelyn was a sympathetic soul. And I felt sorry for her. She seemed to have missed out on a lot in life. I helped her choose some clothes that were more fun than the dull outfits she arrived in and had her redo her hair. And then, when she'd had it cut, I had a dreadful job to persuade her just to come out of her room. I thought I'd have to get her a wig. She was so used to being the drab, middle-aged spinster no one looked at twice, I think she was half-afraid to look attractive. Mutton dressed as lamb, she used to say. But she was still a fetching woman. I'm devastated to hear about her murder. She seemed to be blossoming for the first time.'

'Did you ever visit her in Birtleby?'

'No. She kept that life separate. It wouldn't surprise me if she put back on the dowdy clothes she came in when she went back there. Had a thing about respectability. It must be a narrow-minded town. I don't think I would like to visit it.'

'Did she mention anyone she was afraid of?'

'Not to me. One of her servants terrified her, I think. Someone called Janet. A prim and proper spinster. Evelyn kept going on about how shocked Janet would be if she saw the clothes she'd started wearing, never mind seeing her going about with a young man like me. I think the servants rule some houses.'

'Did she have any other friends here that you know of?'

'No. She did chat with other guests in the hotel, but no one in particular.'

'No other male friends?'

'Modesty isn't one of my stronger features and I have to admit she was fixated on me when I was around. It was flattering, and she wasn't with other men then.'

Very composed, very smooth. Blades supposed Osgood talked his way out of most things, so enjoyed asking him the pointed question, 'Now, if you could oblige us with fingerprints, sir?'

Jack muttered, then checked himself. 'As you wish,' he said.

When that was done, a couple of other vital questions hovered in Blades' brain. 'A nice place you have here, sir.' Jack gave him a questioning glance. 'Are you a man of private means?'

'Yes. My mother left me a considerable sum.'

'And you wouldn't mind telling me the name of your bank?'

Blades wondered how quickly Osgood had been spending it.

# CHAPTER EIGHTEEN

Blades' office was a bare room with a desk, chairs, filing cabinets, walls painted grey 'brightened' by posters of missing persons and a calendar with a photograph of New Scotland Yard, a clutter of papers and files on available surfaces; but it was morning and at least light flooded into it. Blades was wishing it would shed light on the case. He and Peacock were seated round Blades' desk as he looked at papers that Peacock had placed in front of him.

'As you can see, sir, the fingerprints on the poker aren't Jack Osgood's.'

'Inconvenient.'

'And Leeds police have reported in. His alibi checks out. There's no way he could have murdered Miss Wright after Digby left her, then turned up at the Plaza at the time he did.'

'Even less useful.'

'And his bank says his finances are sound, and there are no payments from Evelyn Wright.'

'And that's criminal, though the point of what you're saying is that he isn't. Not on this occasion. It's difficult to just dismiss him though. You'd think a man so much younger – and in her bed – must be after her money at least. And he didn't do it?'

'Perhaps he hadn't got around to it yet?'

'Because someone beat him to it? Well, it won't be some tramp who turned up, killed her, then went away again.'

'I wouldn't be so quick to dismiss tramps,' Peacock said.

'You wouldn't?'

'There are a lot of displaced ex-soldiers around on the road. And they were all trained to kill.'

Blades gave this thought, then grunted. 'It'll be someone with a connection to her, even if we haven't established it yet. And I'm reluctant to give up on Jack Osgood.'

Peacock frowned, then replied, 'Though his alibi does help him.'

'Unfortunately. I suppose we have to forget about him – for the time being.'

'We're sure about everyone else we know had connections with her?'

In reply, Blades started thinking aloud. 'We wondered about Andrew Wright but the only thing we had against him was suspicion, on top of which his alibi checked out and his finances are sound. And we agreed Digby looked likely, but when we went to Leeds, we found out he wasn't the one having the fling with her. The fingerprints on the poker weren't his either, which we haven't found a way past. Which leaves us with who?'

'We haven't got anyone.'

'Unless Osgood found a way of faking that alibi. It's been done before. And just because he's got plenty of money doesn't mean he wouldn't fancy plenty more. He spends enough of it.'

'But there's still the fingerprints,' Peacock said, and his words resounded in the silence that followed.

Blades didn't reply, just frowned and leafed through reports, then stopped at one and smiled. 'But we needn't dismiss him yet.' Blades was looking at a constable's report, which said that a witness had talked to someone asking for Miss Wright on the day of the murder, and the man the witness described sounded much like their own Jack Osgood. This begged the question of why Osgood might have been in Birtleby on the day of the murder. The constable had been asking routine questions of a postman when this had turned up. Blades was glad to have something else on Jack Osgood to check up on. The man was sinister enough and, as his name had cropped up again, it was time, too, that they checked up on whether Osgood had any form. Blades reached for his phone and was soon speaking to London. He put in a request for a search for records, which would be sent up to Birtleby. Then he and Peacock set off to interview the postman.

The local post office was an old brick building in the centre of town. Blades showed his card and asked to see Albert Cummings, the postman who had given the statement. He was in the middle of sorting letters when he was called to the front of the office.

'Alfred Cummings?' Blades asked.

The postman looked up at him with apprehension on his face. 'Yes?' he said.

Blades showed his card again and said he had come to speak to him about the report he had made at the station about the day of Miss Wright's murder. A look of embarrassment came over Albert.

'I wasn't sure whether to mention that or not. And after I did, I wasn't sure I'd done the right thing. My wife nattered on about it. She said there were other women in Birtleby and if any more were murdered it would be my fault for not telling the police what I knew, so there wasn't any way out of it when a policeman came around asking questions. I just had to say. Even if it was the wrong time of day, it couldn't have had anything to do with it, and I don't know. I don't want to be putting some innocent person in a spot.' He took a handkerchief from his pocket and wiped his brow.

'I'm sorry you're being bothered like this, Mr Cummings,' Blades said. 'And you won't be putting anyone in a spot. We check things. We operate on establishing facts, and they can't harm the innocent.'

'I suppose not,' Cummings said, though he did not look convinced. He pulled out a chair and sat down. 'I've been busy this morning, what with delivering mail, collecting it, and sorting it. If they pay you, they think nothing of working you to death, so I'm glad in a way of the chance to stop for a rest.' He laughed, wiped his brow with his handkerchief again, then put it in his pocket. 'Though I wish you were asking me about something else.'

Blades gave Albert a reassuring smile. 'The important thing for us is to have the facts to sift through,' he said. 'Then we can decide whether to dismiss them or not.' But Albert still looked anxious despite his own attempt at a smile. 'I know you told the duty constable all about this when you made your statement, but would you go over it again?'

Albert thought for a moment, sighed, and then began. He began slowly but seemed to gain confidence as he spoke. He seemed to be relieving himself of a burden. 'It was on a Thursday afternoon, the 26th. There's a post-box at the end of Evans Gardens and I was emptying it. I'd unlocked it and taken out the few letters that were there when a man spoke to me, so I turned around. It was the day of the murder, which caused a stir round here, so you can date things by then. And this was that day.'

'Was there anything striking about the man?'

'I'll tell you he was a bit odd. He gave me such a wide smile it quite frightened me, not that it would be supposed to. Apart from that, let's see. He was tall but not as tall as you. How old was he? Mid-twenties? He was a slim man, well put together. Neat hair. Dark brown. He was dressed in quite a dandy suit, a black one, and he had a bright tie, red it was, with a diamond pin in it. I remember that. You don't see that many of them. And he had ever such smart shoes on. You couldn't help but notice them. Black and white patent leather. Not the type of person you come across all that often around here.' Then he stopped, having run out of words.

'What did he say to you?'

'He asked the way to Miss Wright's.'

'Did he say why he wanted to see her?'

'He said a relative of his knew her and he'd been asked to look her up as he was in the area. I pointed out the house to him, and he looked in its direction and nodded. Then I turned around to put the letters in my bag, locked the post-box and continued with my round.'

'Did you notice what he did?'

'He didn't go up to the house which I thought a bit odd, just stood at the gate and stared in its direction. Then he got back in his car and drove off.'

'His car?'

'Did I not mention it?'

'What was that like?'

'Big sporty model. Black.'

'What make?'

Cummings grimaced. 'Couldn't tell you. I know nothing about cars. Horses yes. Cars no.'

It did sound as if it could be Jack Osgood's car, Blades thought, which fitted nicely with the description Cummings had given, and which contradicted what Jack Osgood had said.

'Do you know what time this was?'

'Two o'clock in the afternoon.'

'That sounds precise.'

'That's when I always empty that post-box. That's when it's supposed to be done.'

'And you were on time that day?'

'Yes.'

'You'd never seen him before?'

'He was a stranger to me.'

'Have you seen him again?'

'No.'

'Did anyone else ask you the way to Miss Wright's?'

'Not me. Though anyone could be visiting that house for all I know. I just go past it on my rounds and I don't have time to waste.'

'Thank you, Mr Cummings. You've done your civic duty and you can take pride in it.'

# CHAPTER NINETEEN

Definitely a lounge lizard, thought Blades as he looked across the room at Jack Osgood again. They had tracked him down to a suitably lavish hotel, where he was seated in the restaurant sipping from a gold-rimmed china teacup and talking to a young lady dressed in silk.

Blades had waited till he had sight of Osgood's record when it was sent up from London. It had made interesting reading, and he was glad of the chance to question Jack about it. 'Pleased to meet up with you again, Jack,' Blades said as he drew up a chair to their table and Peacock did the same. 'Good afternoon,' he said to Jack's lady friend, tipping his bowler at her. He gave Jack his own best effort at a charming smile, but, on this occasion, Jack did not give one in return.

'I thought we'd finished discussing that matter,' Jack said.

'Matter? What matter?' the young lady interrupted. 'Who are these men, Jack?'

Blades handed over his card to her as he introduced himself to her. 'Inspector Blades of Yorkshire Constabulary, and this is Sergeant Peacock.' He gave her a smile too.

'The police? What have you been up to, Jack?'

Jack shrugged his shoulders, then simpered at her. 'I haven't been up to anything, Clara. I don't know what this is about.' He now shot an inquiring look at Blades.

'Just some more questions, sir. About the murder of Miss Wright.'

Clara sat back in her seat. She frowned in Jack's direction.

'Tell me he didn't say that, Jack.'

'It's about someone I met once or twice who was found dead in mysterious circumstances, and they're questioning anybody who might have known her even slightly to see if they can give them any information that'll help them catch whoever did it. That's all.' Then he turned to Blades. 'But I don't know anything, which I've told you before.'

'More information has come to light, sir.'

'I don't want to be dragged into anything, Jack,' Clara said as she looked the policemen up and down. She seemed impressed by the seriousness of their demeanour.

'And I don't think Clara's ever met Evelyn Wright at all,' Jack said. 'They don't need to talk to you,' he said to Clara.

'Evelyn Wright, did you say?' Clara said. 'I've heard about her. She was murdered, wasn't she? Why are they asking you about that, Jack?'

Jack now looked nonplussed and seemed to think it wiser to say nothing.

Blades considered Clara. She was attractive, but probably not bright, someone else who might be manipulated by a man like Osgood. 'Your boyfriend did know her,' Blades said.

'But you don't need to speak with me,' Clara said, rising from her seat.

'No. They don't,' Jack said, 'but don't go, Clara. This won't take long.'

'I don't want to get involved,' she said to Jack as she put her wrap over her shoulders. 'We can meet up again some other time. I won't say I was glad to meet you,' she said to Blades and Peacock, 'but do have a good rest of the day.'

'Thank you, ma'am,' Blades said.

Clara turned and left. Jack looked after her then turned to Blades and Peacock. 'You certainly spoiled that little interlude,' he said.

Blades supposed he ought to apologise but did not. 'As I said, sir, new information has come to light.'

'Which is?'

'I didn't know about your record the last time we met?'

'Oh, that.' Jack looked annoyed but dismissive. 'It was some time ago.'

'It's not something small, sir. You were arrested in London for the murder of your mother.'

'And released,' Jack said quickly.

'To recap the whole sorry tale,' Blades went on, 'you were enrolled at university and I daresay you told your mother you went to lectures, but you spent your time at dance halls instead, whooping it up with a variety of young ladies, none of them very light on the wallet. The point being that you paid for this by stealing cheques from your mother and forging them.'

'I was a bit younger then. I would have more sense now.'

'And when your mother found out about this, there was a dreadful row, and a couple of days after that she was found dead, apparently of an overdose of medicine, leaving you a nice size of fortune.'

'I didn't kill her.'

'In despair at her son, she took her own life. That was the official conclusion.'

'As I said, I did not murder her.'

'And you show no remorse for the death of your mother?'

'Why should I? I'm not a murderer.'

'You miss the point. Even if you're not, you were the cause of her death.'

Now Jack simply said nothing, as if he'd realised there was no arguing with Blades.

'You said something about Evelyn being a mother-substitute?' Blades continued. 'And the police seemed to think you murdered your mother even if they couldn't prove it. That doesn't sound good.'

Jack leaned back in his seat and laughed. He took out a cigarette. 'Would you like one, gentlemen?'

'No, thank you, sir,' Blades replied.

'I suppose you wouldn't,' Jack said. 'Well, I will.' He lit his expensive Turkish cigarette, breathed in a lungful of smoke, then slowly exhaled, but he said nothing as he waited for Blades to continue.

'You say you never visited Evelyn in Birtleby?'

'I would have done but she wanted to keep me a secret. I did suggest developing the relationship by seeing each other over there as well, but no. She had one life in Birtleby and one here. She'd been repressed a long time I think, something to do with that father of hers. She was the virtuous spinster who did good works, and she seemed to find it difficult to move on from that image.'

'So, it would surprise you to hear that a witness has placed you in Birtleby?' Peacock asked him. Jack drew in more smoke from his cigarette and gave Peacock a lengthy stare.

'On the day of the murder,' Blades added.

'So, who's this witness?' Jack replied. 'I don't know anyone in Birtleby and I doubt if anyone knows me there.'

'It's not someone who knows you, but it is someone who can describe you – and your car,' Blades said.

'Oh, that.'

'It is distinctive.'

'I suppose it is.'

'And we can do a witness parade.'

'If you wish, but it won't worry me.'

'You stood on Miss Wright's street almost opposite her house and asked for directions to it. Now, why would you do that?'

Jack drew in more smoke. 'I dare say you'll have it out of me,' he said. 'I might as well just tell you. She was a funny sort, Evelyn, so secretive. I was in Leeds, hidden away from everybody in Birtelby, and everybody in Birtleby was hidden away from me. I just wanted to have a look at her place out of curiosity. You never know, she might not have been the lady she made herself out to be. She could have lived in a hovel for all I knew.'

'You wanted to see if she was worth the bother of cultivating?' Peacock said. 'You were checking there was money there to be wheedled out of her?'

'Doesn't say much, your friend, does he?' Jack said to Blades, 'but when he does, he's straight to the point.'

'He's sharp is Sergeant Peacock. That's how I would describe it. And you did get a prison sentence for forgery.'

Jack ignored that remark. 'So I had a quick gander at her house, decided she was probably kosher and drove back to Leeds.'

'And we're supposed to believe that, are we, sir?' Peacock said.

'You'll believe what you decide to,' Jack replied, 'but that's what happened, and I do have an alibi for that evening.'

'We've been looking at Miss Wright's bank accounts,' Blades said. 'There were large withdrawals when she was here in Leeds.'

'Evelyn was bright. She wasn't the sort to leave her chequebook lying around.'

'You checked that, did you, sir?' Peacock said.

There was a flash of anger in Jack's eyes, but he controlled it. 'She did buy me this,' he said and flourished a gold ring.

'Very nice, sir,' Blades said.

'And I encouraged her to buy herself attractive jewellery.'

Blades studied Osgood and took in the note of pomposity. 'And you helped her with her wardrobe too, you said.'

'She was an attractive woman. There was no need for her to dress dowdily. And you'll find her jewellery somewhere in her house I should think, along with the receipts, unless the murderer took it. And that was not me. I suppose you did check my alibi?'

'Oh yes. We checked it, and it stands up. We haven't worked out how you got to Birtleby to do that murder – if that's what you did. But we're going to continue asking questions.'

'You do that,' Jack said.

And that was that. They'd got Jack to agree to what was written in his file, and it would have been difficult for him to do anything else. They'd also learned his excuse for being in Birtleby, which might have been true and might not. But they'd learned nothing new from him, and Blades was disappointed that they hadn't managed to rile him more than they had. This was a cool customer. Or was he just cold?

'Can you tell us about her friends in Birtleby?'

'She didn't talk about them much. I knew about Digby Russell, of course. He struck me as being rather wet, but he might be your man for all that.'

'What makes you say that?'

'Or might not be. I wouldn't know.'

Blades asked Jack some more questions, but deliberately flippant replies betrayed nothing that might be of any help to the investigation.

* * *

'You decided not to arrest him then?' Peacock said as they left.

'On what grounds?' Blades replied. 'Because we've proof he visited Birtleby once?'

'I didn't think you would,' Peacock said.

Blades felt disappointment after the interview but, at the same time, relief. On the one hand, Osgood was a beautiful suspect. He already was a murderer – probably. But what had he earned from Evelyn's death? It was easy to see what he had gained from his mother's death but why kill Evelyn? Blades wondered if he would be like this with every suspect, pleased to be convinced of their innocence. He knew too well that charging someone brought its own problems and he didn't want to go through it lightly. Then a report turned up of another suspect, which drew his mind away and gave him another avenue of investigation.

# CHAPTER TWENTY

It was Constable Wintour who had turned up something. 'Look at this, Peacock,' Blades said, looking at Wintour's report. 'A grocer's boy. You'd think they'd stand a chance of seeing something. Nobody notices them, and they have a habit of turning up unexpectedly. Cavendish's delivery boy. That's the grocer Miss Wright did her regular business with. The boy saw Miss Wright taking a stroll in her back garden with a man much younger than her. And they were holding hands.'

'The respectable Miss Wright at it again?'

'Unless he's making it up, and he could be. Some boys like to feel important. Why didn't any of the servants report this, or the gardener? But we can hardly ignore it. We'll look him up.'

When they entered the grocery shop, they found Mr Cavendish engaged in giving instructions to various white-aproned men and boys who bustled around, fetching this and that for different orders. Mr Cavendish stopped to attend to them.

'You have a delivery boy called Alan Young I believe?' Blades delivered the statement in a clear and authoritative manner and Mr Cavendish's face immediately took on a flustered look. 'I do. What's he done? I'm very strict with my staff. I don't put up with anything.'

'He hasn't done anything wrong. He's done the opposite. He came up with some information that might help us with a case we're working on.'

This didn't appear to cheer up Mr Cavendish who tutted and frowned but then called out to one of the assistants to go and fetch Alan. 'You're in luck,' he said. 'He should be loading up his delivery bike out back right now. What's this got to do with?'

Blades gave him a polite smile but did not reply. Alan appeared, looking perturbed. He was a boy with a ruddy face and alert eyes that darted between Mr Cavendish and Blades before settling on Blades. Blades recapped for him. 'You volunteered some information to Constable Wintour about something you'd witnessed at the Wright house.'

'The Wright case?' Cavendish boomed. 'We've heard all about that. And Alan saw something? Why didn't you come forward with it before this, Alan?'

Blades bit back a sterner comment as he said, 'If you don't mind, sir, if you would leave us alone with Alan, it'll work better that way.'

Cavendish looked disappointed and annoyed but one look at Blades' face told him to comply. 'I've some paperwork to do in the office,' he said and left them to it.

Blades smiled at Alan and put on his most benign expression. 'If you could just tell us what you told Constable Wintour?'

Alan glanced now from Blades to Peacock, then addressed Blades. 'It was a few weeks ago. I was delivering lamb and sausages next door and was running a bit late, so I wasn't hanging about. Then I saw them and that made me stop. It was a sunny day, so I wasn't surprised to see Miss Wright having a stroll in the garden, but she was with someone I'd never seen before, a man. He was younger than her, a lot younger. He had fair hair and a beard. I noticed that in particular. He'd a full-length coat on, navy-blue, oh, and he wore a navy-blue felt hat. And he had a stick; that was black, with a silver handle.'

'You noticed quite a lot, then?'

'I must have gawped a bit. They were holding hands. She was looking at him quite the thing as they chatted away, and I thought, Oh, Miss Wright, who'd have thought it? But I didn't hang about. I had my rounds to do.'

'Was this someone you'd seen before?'

'I've never seen him about.'

'Can you be exact about the date?'

'It was a Tuesday because that's when I do that delivery and it's at about eleven in the morning, but which Tuesday was it? Let's see. Three weeks ago.'

Well before the murder then, Blades thought. 'I don't suppose you heard anything they were saying?'

'I was too far away for that.'

Blades supposed he'd found out what he'd come to discover. 'Thanks for your help,' he said. 'You've already given your statement to Constable Wintour, so you don't need to give another one. You've been a good lad. It's a pity there aren't more like you.'

This pleased Alan who preened himself.

As they left the grocer's shop, Peacock said, 'He's telling the truth, sir.'

Blades grinned back at him. 'Undoubtedly. There are too many details for it to be anything else.'

'And the man he saw is neither Digby nor Osgood.'

'No.'

'Do you think we've found the owner of the prints on the poker at last?'

Blades was feeling hopeful of that but reminded himself it might not turn out to be the case. 'If we can find him, we'll get the answer to that,' he said.

'How do we do that?'

'We release a press statement.'

# CHAPTER TWENTY-ONE

The article that appeared in *The Birtleby Times* was less sensational than might have been expected, as if the writer was himself shocked at reporting such a crime in Birtleby.

## SUSPECT SOUGHT FOR THE MURDER OF MISS WRIGHT

*The investigation into the murder of Miss Evelyn Wright on Thursday, 26 July continues. Some information has come to light since the discovery of her body in the drawing room at her mansion in Birtleby at Evans Gardens. The police still seek the person who left Miss Wright with gashes on her forehead from a fire iron left on the rug beside her in front of her drawing-room fire. Who did she struggle with? Things had been thrown around, but there was no sign of a break-in and nothing was taken. The police think the attacker was probably known to Miss Wright. So far there are no major suspects but the police wish to interview a man described by one of the witnesses. He is a young man, in his twenties or thirties, has fair hair and a beard, is said to be well-dressed, and has been seen wearing a navy-blue, full-length coat and a navy-blue felt hat. He carries a black stick with a silver top. If anyone knows who this might be, could they please get in touch with the police at Birtleby? The police would be grateful for anyone with further information to come forward.*

'It might help,' Peacock said.

'I'm not sure how else we can find him,' Blades said. 'And there must be witnesses around who saw something else useful. Perhaps we'll get more people coming forward, just as long as it's not attention-seekers.'

'It's amazing,' Peacock said. 'Someone walks unobserved into a house, commits a murder, and departs without leaving traces or being seen leaving.'

'It's what we're left with. Of the people we know were there, none of their prints fits, not even the servants'. In any case, I don't see the motive for any of them.'

'She travelled about in Leeds,' Peacock said.

'Yes,' Blades replied. 'We could publicise it in a Leeds newspaper too.'

# CHAPTER TWENTY-TWO

The article was helpful because some people did come forward with useful information, and a clerk from the railway station turned up at the police station. Sergeant Ryan was on duty.

Sergeant Ryan was not only the regulation six foot, but he was broad. As he was in his mid-forties now, a lot of his bulk was padded and comfortable, but he knew he still looked ominous and often played on it, though it could be a disadvantage on desk duty. Today he noticed that the man approaching the desk visibly quaked, even though Ryan had given him his official welcoming smile. The clerk, Philip Middleton, was five feet two and, being sedentary in his habits, was not a muscular man. Visibly nervous, he turned as if to leave again. The sergeant coughed as if in apology.

'Can I help you, sir?' he said in a tone as mild as possible.

Philip stopped, thought for a moment, then turned around again.

'I suppose as I've come this far,' he muttered.

'What's the problem, sir?'

'Well, it's this.' Philip paused as if losing his nerve again, then continued, 'It's in answer to that newspaper article.'

'Yes, sir?'

'The one about the murder of Miss Wright. You asked if anyone had seen a man answering a certain description?'

'We did.' Sergeant Ryan's eyes were keen as he looked at Philip Middleton now.

'I've seen him. I'm a clerk at the railway station. I saw him when he arrived in Birtleby and when he left.'

'You're sure it's him?'

'He fitted the description.' Philip started to look more relaxed, even relieved as he unburdened himself. 'He came off the Leeds train. As the paper said, he was young, about medium height, wearing the exact clothes they described, and carrying that cane. Definitely not from around here. It was a southern accent he had.'

'When was this, sir?'

'A few weeks ago. Maybe three weeks. Yes. That would be right. Not the night of the murder. I don't see how he's connected to Miss Wright's death, but he did ask the way to the house.'

'Miss Wright's house?'

'That's what I'm saying. He said he was a cousin who'd always meant to look her up and he happened to be nearby.'

'He came off the Leeds train?'

'The nine o'clock. And he went back on the three o'clock I think it was.'

'Did you see his ticket?'

'I had to check that. It was a return ticket all the way from Leeds.'

'Not just passing then, unless he'd other business in Birtleby. How did he seem?'

'I don't know really. I didn't pay much attention when he arrived. He was just another customer asking a question. I noticed him more when he was on his way back. He was cheerful as if something had gone well.'

'Did he speak to you?'

'He just kept himself to himself, but he was whistling as he stood about waiting for his train. I couldn't help noticing that.'

'And you'd recognize him again?'

'Oh yes.'

'That's helpful, sir. If you'd care to make a statement, I'll pass it on to Inspector Blades when he returns.' Sergeant Ryan concealed his excitement, but he did expect this would be important.

* * *

Another member of the public came forward with useful information, a local lady called Mrs Isobel Wharton. She was a large person with a wide, sweeping, feathered hat, who was wearing a red fox-fur collar. She had a look of steel in her eye and her demeanour, and she certainly did not look the sort of person to be intimidated by overgrown police sergeants.

'You asked for information,' she boomed. 'In your newspaper article about poor Evelyn's death, about a certain person, and gave a description. I'm here about that.'

Suitably deferential, Sergeant Ryan replied. 'It's very good of you to come forward, madam. What information do you have for us?' He asked the question punctiliously even though something about her did make him nervous.

Isobel picked at her fox collar. Unsatisfied with it somehow, she took it off, then threw the fox's head behind her as she swung the fur into a more comfortable position round her shoulders. By then, Sergeant Ryan supposed, she had worked out the content of her speech. 'I knew Evelyn well,' Isobel continued, 'from when she was such a keen member of the Methodists. We were on a committee together, so I would recognise Evelyn anywhere. And it was because of where I'd known her from that she surprised me. I was on a train to Catterick in the Dales when I saw her. She was on it too, with a young man. This was a few months ago. I was there with my children. My husband was supposed to be with us as well, but something had cropped up in his business. When I spotted her, I couldn't believe what I was seeing. She was standing looking doe-eyed at this young man, young enough to be her son, and he was looking back at her, equally struck.'

Isobel started playing with her collar unconsciously again and Sergeant Ryan studied the hand movements.

'He did have the fair hair it said in the newspaper,' she continued, 'and blue eyes, and this neat little beard, fair as well. I didn't know whether to acknowledge her or not. Anyway, I got off at Catterick and she remained on the train and that's all there is to my story. I hadn't thought it worth bothering you with, but my husband thought any information could help you. After all, somebody murdered her, and you don't know who, and you'll want to know something about the kind of people she was associating with. But I've no idea who he was. I'd never seen him before and I've never seen him again.' She played with the collar again but left it in place.

'Would you recognize him if you did?'

'I don't see why not. I had a good look at him. I was curious.'

'Thank you for the information ma'am. It sounds invaluable. Now, can I ask you to make a statement?'

'Of course, young man.' It surprised Sergeant Ryan to be called this as no one had said that to him in years. 'That's why I came.'

Various other people appeared at Sergeant Ryan's desk in answer to the newspaper article, and Ryan duly listened and took statements, but most were inconsequential and a lot unlikely. Ryan did not see any of them were going to make it easier for Blades and Peacock to locate the man they were looking for.

# CHAPTER TWENTY-THREE

Blades and Peacock were seated in the manager's office at The Princess Grand, which had been loaned to them for the occasion. Peacock held his notebook in his hand as usual. The room wasn't as opulent as the rest of the hotel, though it still boasted striped blue and gold wallpaper and a majestic oak desk; there were no gilt-framed pictures, just a board with staff notices, and the carpet showed signs of wear.

The young man seated in front of them was about eighteen, sallow, thin, and with eyes that shifted here, there and everywhere. That did suggest unreliability to Blades but he checked himself. It would be a mistake to pre-judge the witness.

Word had gone around the hotel about the line of questioning Blades had been following during his previous visit, and it had occurred to this young man that he might know something the police would be interested in. After taking his statement, Leeds police had phoned up Blades.

Len Hodgkins' eyes settled on Blades as he started to speak. 'I wasn't on last week when you were at the hotel questioning staff and I'm sorry I didn't come forward earlier than this.'

'You have now,' Blades said. He smiled and waited for the witness to continue.

'I need my job here. It can be difficult to get one and you don't want to call attention to yourself.' He indicated his helplessness with a movement of his shoulders.

'So you served Miss Wright?'

'She was here about a month, not that I'm always on as I say. I wish I'd more shifts. I served her maybe seven, eight times. No. It must have been more than that. I dunno.'

'And did she eat alone, or did she have company?'

'That Jack Osgood, I saw her with him a few times.'

'How do you know his name?'

'Everyone knows Jack Osgood. He's loud. He talks to everybody. And a right lad for the ladies they say. Nobody thought Miss Wright was his one and only, whatever she might have thought.'

'We were aware she knew him, but confirmation is useful.'

'There's not much I can add to what you probably know but there were no words between them, not when I was there. I can tell you how smarmy he was and how much she drank it up. She was flattered with him being so much younger, I should think, which probably isn't new to you either. But there is something else I thought you might not know.'

Blades nodded to Peacock who made a show of his readiness to ply his pen.

'There was another bloke with her one time. He was someone I'd seen around the hotel before. I sometimes noticed him talking to some of the wealthier looking residents. When you heard them speaking about him, some said they were a bit doubtful of him. He had some shares he was trying to sell – in a mine in South America – if it exists. He didn't look like the sort you would want to buy shares from, not without doing a lot of checking.'

'Can you describe him?'

'He's a young man. Maybe anyone in trousers could talk Miss Wright into anything or thought they could.'

'Young, you say? About how young?'

'Older than me. Mid to late twenties? And a fit-looking fellow. Had an odd smile, but Miss Wright lapped it up.'

'How tall was he?'

'About five nine? Thereabouts. And he had fair hair, combed back, short, neat. And a close-cut beard. It was blonde too. His accent wasn't from around here. Somewhere southern I would say. Cockney maybe. He laughed a lot, and he had this really loud laugh, particularly when he was laughing at his own jokes. He was a smug know-it-all, not the sort of person I take to, but women seemed to like him, especially that Miss Wright, though I only saw her with him the once.'

'About when was this?'

The waiter thought about this, shook his head, then thought again. 'Second week in June? Yes, it would have been then. The same day as my brother's birthday, June the 10th. I can place it by that.'

'Did you hear anything they spoke about?'

'He didn't half pile on the compliments. I thought, she'll never believe that, but she seemed to. Looked like a cat that had got the cream. He told her she didn't look a day over thirty, and if he'd said fifty I'd have found it believable.'

'So he flattered her?'

'And he did take out papers at one point. Would have been to do with those shares he was usually trying to sell I suppose. She looked at them, then just put them to the side. It was him she was interested in, but how the conversation developed beyond that, I couldn't say. I had a lot of tables to wait on.'

'Did you make out his name?'

'It was Renshaw, Peter Renshaw.'

'You're sure of that?'

'Oh yes. He's well known around here.'

'He is? Do you know where we can find him?'

'Didn't I say? He's the Sales Manager at the Ford garage in Camberwell Lane.'

Blades and Peacock grinned at each other.

# CHAPTER TWENTY-FOUR

Mr Peter Renshaw fitted the description of their suspect exactly, with his wispy fair hair and neatly trimmed beard, and Blades and Peacock were seated opposite him now, pretending to be interested in buying a Model T Ford. Renshaw had on his work suit, but it was of a reasonable quality, and he wore a striking tie in a lurid purple and black with a silver tiepin set in the centre of it. At a push, you might describe him as well-dressed. They could vouch for his charm as he prattled on about the technicalities of the engine, the rpm and the comfort of the leather upholstery, his gushing enthusiasm as eloquent as his words. Blades soon realised that the only way to get out of a test drive would be to show his police card, even if the drive would be fun.

But, for now, Blades contented himself with asking questions. 'Have you been with this firm long?'

'Quite some time. I started off as a salesman but worked my way up.' He sat further back in his seat with a self-satisfied smile as he started to boast. 'I've improved business no end. This showroom is twice the size it was before I was promoted. Sales up every year. Profits up. My wife's father is the brother-in-law of the owner.' Blades tried to work out that relationship while Renshaw continued. 'But he has nothing to complain about. I've made the most of the opportunity. Now the Model T Ford. You must view it properly.'

'I'd like nothing better,' Blades said, 'but–' And it was then that he produced his card. 'Unfortunately, it isn't the Model T Ford I'm interested in.'

'But I thought you said–'

'I didn't. You assumed it, sir, because I talked about cars when I first approached you, and it's a topic worth addressing but it isn't what I'm here for.'

'Are you investigating the showroom? Why?'

'No, sir. I'm here to ask questions about you. You know how it is. The police receive information and follow it up. The information we get is supposed to be helpful, but that's what I'm here to establish. Now, if you don't mind answering a few questions.'

The peeved expression on Peter's face was the opposite of charm. 'If I must,' he said. He took out a cigarette without offering one to either Blades or Peacock, leaned back in his chair and waited. Blades now noticed the solid gold cufflinks and the silver-monogrammed cigarette lighter. Perhaps this Renshaw was better turned out than he'd given him credit for.

'Do you ever visit Birtleby?'

There was a tightening of the lips but otherwise Renshaw answered evenly. 'I've been there with my wife and nippers once or twice. A visit to the seaside.'

'Have you ever been there on your own?'

'No.'

'You weren't there on the evening of Thursday, July the 26th?'

Renshaw didn't answer but took a long draw from his cigarette before saying. 'What's significant about that date?'

'Were you there then?'

'I don't know what you think I've done but I haven't done anything.' He pointed a finger at Blades. 'I know what you think of me. I dress well but I'm a working-class type. You look in my direction and think I should have done something criminal. My accent's all wrong. But all I do is work and work hard. Graft has got me where I am. I've as much to be proud of as anybody.'

Blades noticed the vigour in the bluster, but also that Renshaw hadn't answered the question. He decided to wait for him to do that.

Renshaw scratched his nose, took another draw on his cigarette, then said, 'Let's see. That's over a week ago now. I've no idea what I was doing then, but I wasn't in Birtleby. I've never been there on my own.' Which was a simple answer and Blades thought it odd that Renshaw had taken so long to give it, though Renshaw seemed less worried now for some inexplicable reason. 'Oh, yes, I was at home all evening.'

'Can your wife confirm this?'

'She was out at her mother's and had the children with her, so she can't.'

'Leaving you on your own?'

'I was doing paperwork for this place. There's a lot of it.'

'But no one can confirm you were at home that evening?'

Renshaw took another draw of his cigarette as he considered. 'No.'

'Did you know Miss Wright?'

'Who?'

'Miss Evelyn Wright of Elmwood Hall, Birtleby.'

Renshaw now had a look of what seemed forced nonchalance on his face. 'No.'

Blades said, 'I see.' He watched Renshaw drum his fingers on the arm of his chair. 'Well, I've asked you as much as I need to for the moment.' He allowed the words 'for the moment' to linger.

'So, what was this information you received?' Renshaw asked him.

'I'm sorry, sir. That's confidential. Oh, and can you give me your home address? And, as nobody can confirm your alibi as you've agreed, you won't mind if Sergeant Peacock takes your fingerprints, will you?'

When Blades and Peacock departed, they left a harassed Peter Renshaw still attempting to look careless.

# CHAPTER TWENTY-FIVE

Philip Middleton, the railway station clerk, had always avoided police stations and here he was in one for the second time. It was a gloomy enough place, with its bare, whitewashed walls and linoleum floors. Philip was sitting in a waiting room while they assembled the suspects. Well, one of them was the suspect but they had said they would round up more who looked similar.

The door opened, and a constable walked in. 'Thank you for waiting, Mr Middleton. The line-up is ready now, so if you would just come through.'

Philip had felt so sure before but, in all the time he had been sitting there, had not been able to recall an image of the man he'd seen, and Philip wondered if he was going to be any help at all. He had not realised at the time what offering information would lead to, and he was wishing he had never said anything. When he stood up to follow the constable, he was not sure for a moment whether his legs were going to do what they were told but was very glad when they did.

The men were standing in a row side by side and facing forwards. To Philip's relief, there were also two policemen in the room. Philip had been told to put his hand on the shoulder of the person he recognized and was nervous about the reaction he might receive. The men were on the other side of the room from where Philip entered, so Philip had a general look at all of them before the constable who had brought him in signalled to him to walk in front of the men one by one to study them.

'Please walk forward now, sir.'

So he did. They were all dressed in a similar fashion: in jackets that fitted in with Philip's description of what the man he had seen had been wearing at the ticket office. The first man was nonchalant as he stared ahead of him as Philip assumed the police had instructed him to be. Philip would not have described that man's hair as fair but a shade of brown, so he knew this was not him. The second man was stout. The third was too tall. The fourth was the right height and weight, had the correct colour of hair, and it lay across his forehead in the way that Philip remembered. The fifth was the right height, weight, and again had the correct colour of hair, but also had a squint. The sixth was the wrong age. Philip supposed the police had done their best to get a line-up of men who fitted the description but, as far as he was concerned, there was only one man who looked anything like the man he had seen. Philip stood in front of the fourth suspect again, looked him up and down, and tried to think of anything that was not right. He did fit what Philip remembered but he still hesitated. There was something. What was it? Oh yes. The eyes. Had they been blue? He cast his mind back and tried to picture again the man he had seen. To his relief, a picture came, but the eyes were unclear in it. Had they been blue or grey? He supposed that after that length of time he could have become unsure about anything. Trust your gut feeling, a voice inside him said and, apparently unbidden, his right hand rose and placed itself on the suspect's shoulder.

* * *

Blades and Peacock were seated watching the parade when Philip picked out Renshaw and they were delighted at this. This was, however, only the first part of the identification process. There were two other witnesses who would walk up and down in front of these men and say yea or nay. The constables had kept the other witnesses apart before the parade and would keep them separated after they had done their parts. The men stood in their line-up silent and tense, still under the instructions of the two policemen in the room. Then the next witness was brought in.

Isobel Wharton was still wearing the mistreated but fortunately dead fox fur around her neck as she strode into the room. Her eyes glanced everywhere before settling on the men in their uneven row. Then they slowly swept from one end of the line to the other as they condemned what they were looking at. When motioned to, she stepped forward then strode along beside them. She scrutinised the men, who still looked ahead, and did their best to avoid meeting her gaze. She stopped twice. She stared at the eyes of the fifth man, shook her head, made to walk on, changed her mind and stepped back in front of him again. She made as if to raise her hand to put it on his shoulder, then shook her head and walked back in front of the fourth man. After gazing for what seemed a remarkable length of time she nodded and placed her hand on his shoulder with such decisiveness that the man winced with the contact. Then she looked at the constable who had led her in, he nodded, and she proceeded to leave the room.

Blades and Peacock glanced at each other again with satisfied looks on their faces. Renshaw had now been picked out twice. They were able to place him in Birtleby due to Philip Middleton's testimony, where, according to Philip, he had been asking the way to Miss Wright's house which showed a connection with her. Isobel's testimony proved more. She had seen Renshaw with Evelyn on that train to Catterick when they had been behaving like lovers, which suggested a very close connection. One witness to go. How would this work out?

With his skinny frame, Alan Young looked his fourteen years, and out of place in this adult situation. He did as he was directed by the constable and was soon walking up the line, though he did that at no great pace. He looked at every man in the line-up with an anxious expression as if he might be put in prison himself if he got this wrong. Everyone was given the same length of stare, no one dismissed quickly. Blades did wonder if the boy was going to chicken out. Then Alan Young moved up to the constable and whispered with him. The constable nodded, and Alan walked past the line-up again. This was no quick fly-past either, but a sequence of concentrated gazes. Alan turned, strode back to the fourth man, and placed his hand on his shoulder. He did not leave it there long, but the gesture had been clear enough. Blades sighed, and there was relief in it.

'That places him in Evelyn's garden, and we have him holding hands with her,' Peacock gloated.

'It'll be interesting to hear what Renshaw says about what he told us. Everything he said is cobblers. He has been in Birtleby on his own and he did know Miss Wright.'

# CHAPTER TWENTY-SIX

Renshaw was seated in the interview room at Birtleby Station with its bare walls and floor, the only furniture a desk and chairs. Blades reflected that Renshaw did have a distinctive appearance with that wispy blonde beard, but, as he looked at his bleak stare, noted that there was nothing of the perky and natty about him now. To the right of Blades sat Peacock, notebook in hand, pencil ready.

'You've been telling us lies, sir,' Blades said to Renshaw. Renshaw grunted, which Blades took to mean disgust at what Blades had said, not agreement with it. Blades continued. 'You may be wondering who the witnesses were who identified you at the identification parade?'

Renshaw snorted now, then said, 'I've never seen any of them before.'

'The first one was a clerk from Birtleby Railway Station. In your statement, you said that, apart from a couple of day visits to the beach with your wife and children, you'd never been to Birtleby. The clerk identified you as arriving from Leeds and returning from the station to Leeds on your own.'

In a discomfited voice, Renshaw said, 'Perhaps it was someone who looked a bit like me.'

'But the boy who identified you also saw you in Birtleby. He saw you in Miss Wright's gardens walking hand in hand with her, a person you said you did not know.'

Renshaw looked away. He scratched behind his ear, looking as if he were giving thought to something, stopped, then gave Blades a glare. 'On the basis of seeing this person once, obviously from a distance, he's confident about identifying me? He's a boy. They tell stories to feel important.'

'And our third witness, definitely not a boy, places you on a day's outing to Catterick, on a train with Miss Wright, extremely close and particularly enjoying each other's company.'

'Catterick isn't Birtleby, is it?'

Though Renshaw's tone was sharp, Blades thought he saw a more relaxed look in the eyes. He assumed this was because what the witnesses had said did not sound as damning as Renshaw had thought it would. So that meant he had been expecting to be placed in Birtleby on the night of the murder?

Blades persisted. 'Our witness states that on May the 5th she saw you on that train with Miss Wright. Were you?'

'No.'

Renshaw's tone had now become dismissive, which annoyed Blades.

'Can you tell us where you were then?'

'Not offhand. No.'

'Does your work take you away from home?'

'Sometimes.'

'Is there a diary you can check? We can arrange to have your work diaries brought here.'

Renshaw muttered something indistinct, thought for a moment, then replied, 'Let's see. I think I might remember. Yes. That's it. A sales conference in Harrogate.'

'No doubt you have receipts that show this?'

'I don't know.'

'I'm sure you put in expenses claims, sir.' Renshaw looked nonplussed. 'Did you go by yourself or did you have a secretary with you?'

'I was by myself.'

'As you were at a sales conference, no doubt you can produce witnesses?'

Renshaw's face now showed a mind working its way through a problem with difficulty. 'I did travel to Harrogate, but I was ill on the day of the conference.'

Blades was disappointed as he'd expected Renshaw to be sharper. 'What was the name of the hotel you stayed in, sir?'

'The Swan Hotel.' This was said quickly but Blades noticed a new uncertainty in the tone. Then with a sneer, Renshaw said, 'You'll check, no doubt?'

'Oh, yes, sir.'

Renshaw shifted in his seat. He put his hand up to his mouth and chewed a thumbnail, became aware of this then put his hand back on the arm of his chair, where his fingers seemed to drum of their own volition. Then he stopped himself doing that. Not quite so relaxed now, Blades thought. There was a forlornness in Renshaw's defiance as he replied, 'So you'll check.' Then he shifted forward in his seat as something occurred to him. 'Shouldn't I have a lawyer?'

'You're not being charged with anything, sir. We're asking questions, that's all, but we can arrange a lawyer for you if you wish.'

'I know what they cost.' Renshaw looked gloomy at the thought. Then he seemed to brighten up. 'Anyway, I haven't done anything. You'll get bored and let me go.' He sat back in his chair in a renewed display of insouciance.

'Your alibi for the night of Miss Wright's murder,' Blades continued. 'It's weak. You said you were alone in your house all evening doing paperwork, but no one can confirm that.' Now Renshaw appeared to have decided not to reply. 'The obvious explanation for not having any witnesses is that you were in Birtleby doing the murder.'

In answer, Renshaw glared at something just to the side of Blades' head.

Blades continued to press. 'Your alibi for your Catterick trip isn't going to hold up either, is it, sir?' But Renshaw kept to his decision.

Blades' voice adopted a softer tone as he continued with his questioning. It didn't do any harm and it might help make Renshaw drop his guard. 'It's not a crime to know Miss Wright but you won't admit you did. Why?'

Renshaw put an expression on his face that was as blank as he could manage, Blades supposed.

'Let's assume for the moment, unlikely as it may seem, that our three witnesses are wrong, you're still not giving convincing alibis. Is there something else you're covering up? If you're having an affair with someone, that's not a crime, and we're not morally bound to tell your wife, but if a mistress did come forward, it would help you out.' Blades did consider this a possibility, and if it was the truth, he did want to uncover it, but Renshaw still said nothing, as he and Blades sat and stared at each other.

Then Renshaw said, 'If there's nothing else, can I go now?'

Blades gave him his sternest look, then said, 'There's the small matter of your police record. You remember the embezzlement?' Blades had been waiting for the right moment to play this card. He'd been pleased when Peacock had turned this up. Peacock himself had been grinning with pleasure as he laid a file on Blades' desk and told him about the year and a half Renshaw had done for stealing from a firm he had been working for. Blades doubted if the owner of the garage where Renshaw now worked knew about it, and as far as Blades was concerned, it made Renshaw into a real grade A suspect. Now, as prepped, Peacock took over the interview.

'You were eighteen at the time, sir, and working where?'

Renshaw tried defiance again. 'I'm sure my file tells you.'

'Still, if you would recap for us?'

Renshaw groaned. His voice now loud and showing real frustration, he said, 'All right. It was in Croydon at a department store where I worked. As you said, I was very young. I was eighteen and not only broke but in debt. I'd taken up with some mates who were dead keen on the ponies and I dropped a ton at the racecourse. The gossip about the bookie I was in hock to was that he wasn't averse to breaking a few limbs to get what was owed to him – and he was threatening to, so I stole money from the store. I was caught. I did my time. You're not thinking of charging me for that again, are you?'

'Obviously not, sir.'

'Look I was young. I made a mistake. I know better now. I value the job I have. I don't want to lose it.'

'Saying you were only eighteen doesn't cut it though, does it, sir?' Peacock said. 'You were an adult, old enough to know better, as you found out. You were sent to prison for that. And it shows the eye for the main chance. I bet you've still got that, haven't you?'

Now Blades broke in. 'You don't know better, do you, sir? You're going around selling mining shares!'

'Who told you that?' Renshaw asked, looking even more alarmed.

'Which is all right as long as there's a real mine,' Blades continued. 'Is there?'

'Mining shares,' Renshaw groaned as he gathered his thoughts. 'Look, it's a favour for a friend. He asked me to help him out, that's all. Of course, there's a real mine.'

'In Argentina?'

'Yes,' Renshaw replied, but his voice held less conviction.

'I dare say you still have some of those shares in your possession that we can inspect?'

'Not with me, no.'

'Don't worry. We will get a search warrant for your house. We'll also have your bank accounts checked. What is the name of your bank?'

Reluctantly, Renshaw told him.

'Were you ingratiating yourself to Miss Wright, to extract money from her?'

'I don't know her. Now have you finished?'

'You're an attractive enough young man. What else would you see in a woman her age but an opportunity to get at her money?'

'I don't know. I've never met her.'

Blades was disappointed the defiance was still so strong, if not surprised. However, he did think they would probably get him for fraud. But he decided they had probably found out from him as much as they would for now.

# CHAPTER TWENTY-SEVEN

What happened next put all thought of Renshaw out of Blades' mind. He found himself standing and inspecting another body, which lay in the centre flower bed at Elmwood Hall, where it had flattened some purple lupins, though that was the least of anyone's worries. Blades recognized the body, even if the head was a crumpled mess. It was that of a man about forty, broad, of a muscular build, who had been a healthy physical specimen till the garden spade that now lay beside him had clattered him a few times, and it was Charlie Falconer. The murder of Miss Wright, Blades knew, had been done in one clinical blow with a follow-up just to make sure, by someone calm enough to be clear about exactly what they intended. This looked as if it had been done by someone in a frenzy. Or Charlie had shown more reluctance to die.

Charlie was in his work clothes with a basket beside him half full of the weeds he had taken out. He must have been leaning forward, eyes focussed on the task, when the murderer came up behind him. Dr Parker was leaning over Charlie now. He straightened himself up and sighed. 'No more than two hours ago, possibly less.'

'And we received the call about an hour ago.'

'So your murderer isn't long gone.'

'If he's gone.'

As Parker began to replace his instruments in his bag, Blades continued to look at the body. The sight of someone murdered was always a physical shock. A life ended on someone else's whim was both unnatural and shudderingly final. And in the middle of a case. Should he have foreseen this? Should he have prevented this?

'The cause of death is obvious enough?' he asked Parker as he fought to keep the tone of his voice as policeman-like as the question.

'Oh, yes. Killed with blows to the head by an instrument that could be a shovel, just like that.' Dr Parker pointed.

'There is blood on it.'

'The blows weren't carefully aimed, but the killer managed to land the decisive blow in the end.'

'Do the type of blows tell us anything about the murderer?'

'Someone strong enough to wield a spade with intent. A man or a woman used to hard work. Whoever it was, they fairly leathered him. As he would have been leaning down to weed when he was initially struck, you can't judge the height of the assailant, and both hands would have been used to wield the shovel.'

'Someone in a frenzy or just a lot of ill-placed blows?'

'That I can't say. Either or both.'

'Sergeant Peacock has already tested for fingerprints,' Blades said. 'That's twice our murderer has been kind enough to leave the murder weapon beside the body, but he was wearing gloves this time, so he was thinking clearly enough for that.'

'Our murderer learns as he goes along?'

'Probably,' Blades agreed. 'He left clear enough prints all over that poker. There are other prints on the shovel that are good enough, but I'll bet you ten to one, they're Charlie Falconer's.'

'I can't help you with that. I'll arrange for an ambulance to take him to the morgue. Then I'll type up my report and schedule the post-mortem. And I'll leave you to it.'

Peacock had already taken photographs of the body, but Blades told him to keep his camera handy as they looked around. Blades wondered where the murderer had attacked his victim from. He had Peacock take photographs of the general area from every angle. Whoever it was had tried to obliterate prints from their footwear by kicking away at earth, and none of the scuff marks looked particularly helpful. There were marks that looked as if they were from the serrated print of a Wellington boot but there was nothing like a full print. A general idea of size might be worked out with a closer inspection and some measuring.

Blades supposed that, if the murderer came up on Falconer from behind, which he seemed to have done, he would have approached from the area of the house, though that did not mean he had come from inside it. Blades and Falconer walked along the line he might have come from and, though there were signs of passage, there were no clear traces. The murderer had dropped no cigarette or handkerchief, but they would have constables going over this whole area on hands and knees to double-check.

Blades wondered what the motive was this time. There would be nothing to be inherited from a gardener, nor would he be expected to be carrying anything of value. Perhaps Charlie had quarrelled with someone. His wife? It was difficult to see how an arthritic spouse could have done this even if there had been a rift in his marriage. Did it have anything to do with the first murder? Did Falconer know something about that? This was the garden of the house where Miss Wright had been murdered. It was to be expected that two murders in the same place and about the same time would be connected. Did Falconer know something about the man seen walking with Miss Wright in these grounds and identified as Renshaw? Had he seen something on the night of the murder he hadn't talked with them about? Would he be stupid enough to try to blackmail someone? Did he know more about Miss Wright and someone wanted to silence him for that? There were a lot of questions, too many. But the first thing to do after leaving the murder scene under the guard of a constable was to interview the widow.

# CHAPTER TWENTY-EIGHT

The gardener's cottage was a humble affair. Blades could see damp under the sitting-room windowsill suggesting the window had needed replacing for some time, and he noticed that the interior walls were whitewashed stone. The floor consisted of floorboards painted a deep brown and covered here and there with worn rugs. The room was made more personal with prints and photographs on the wall, and there was a pair of china dogs on the wooden mantlepiece.

Margaret Falconer welcomed them in, sat them down, and insisted on them having tea and cake. She said they would need it after what they had been doing. She would have been in her forties, Blades supposed, though she seemed worn down and older. Her face was well lined, with pain from her arthritis, and her hair was as grey as that of a woman in her sixties. She was struggling as she moved about with that stick, but she was so earnestly obliging, that Blades, used to refusing refreshments in these circumstances, was now sitting in a worn, wooden-armed but upholstered seat by the fire with Peacock seated opposite him as they waited for their refreshments.

'Would you like any help with that?' Blades called through to the kitchen after she had lumbered into it.

'Maybe with carrying it through,' her voice replied. 'I'll tell you when it's ready.'

In time, Peacock went through and reappeared with her, carrying a tray with a teapot, floral cups and saucers, with side-plates for the cake that Peacock then had to go back and fetch along with the sugar and milk. Mrs Falconer poured and served, then sat down on her settee, and it was as if that bustling about had kept her going because now she burst into tears. Her head was in her hands as she wept. Blades and Peacock had no idea what to do about this though they had the deepest sympathy for her. They just had to wait till she stopped.

'I'm sorry you've had such bad news, Mrs Falconer,' Blades said.

Then she sobbed again but, after a struggle, managed to recover herself, sat up straight and gave Blades the weakest of smiles.

'Thank you,' she said. 'It's been a shock. He was supposed to be coming in for something to eat and he didn't. It was when I opened the door and looked out to see if he was about, that I saw him lying there.' Then another sob erupted. 'He was covered in blood.' She sobbed again. 'Who would do such a thing? Charlie never hurt anybody.'

'Do you know if he had enemies?' Blades was concentrating on watching the expression on the face of the person he was interviewing so his sipping of tea was automatic, and his consumption of cake was occasional. Peacock seemed pleased by the quality of both, and to have worked up a bit of thirst and hunger. Mrs Falconer didn't touch a thing.

'Charlie didn't have enemies. He never spoke of any. We've been married twenty-five years and I would know. He didn't quarrel with anyone, even when he should have done.'

Blades thought back to his first impression of Charlie and did wonder at the truth of what she was saying.

'Are you able to notice much that's going on up at the house? You don't go out much, do you?'

'I did like it when Charlie kept me company in the garden and I could enjoy the scent of the roses.' Then Blades could see her face beginning to break up, but she did not burst into tears this time. 'I could see plenty from there, but I was never part of it and, of course, I was never in the house, so I can't tell you much about what goes on in there. I can see out of my windows. I might notice someone going in or out because of the view there is from them, but I'm not looking out all day. I could miss anything.'

'Did you happen to notice anyone unusual about the place today, or was anyone from the house going about the gardens?'

'No. I wish I could be more helpful. I'm sorry.'

Blades had not expected her to be witness to anything, but he had asked. On the other hand, she might have heard about something. 'Did your husband talk about Miss Wright's murder with you?'

'It was quite a topic around here. Of course.'

'Was there something worrying him? Was there something he might have seen or heard and that he maybe thought he should tell us about?'

'He didn't know anything. If he had, he would have told me. The first he knew about the murder was when he heard about it on the day the body was discovered by Mary. He was at home with me the night it happened.'

'He didn't mention hearing anybody say something about the night of the murder that might have been useful to us?'

'Not that he told me.'

Margaret Falconer was the possessor of a remarkable lack of information so far, but Blades thought he might as well ask a couple of questions about Renshaw in case the murder was linked to him.

'A witness came forward to tell us of seeing Miss Wright walking about the garden arm in arm with a young man. Do you know anything about that? Did your husband tell you anything?'

'Miss Wright? With a young man? She'd run a mile. I can't imagine such a thing at all. More's the pity. I did hear there was a lot of interest in her from young men when she was younger herself, which was a while ago. I'm sure Miss Wright had given up any thought of such things.'

'You never saw a fair-haired young man about the place? With a beard the same colour?'

'Someone's been spinning you a tale. There's been no one like that within a mile of Miss Wright's place.'

Blades was disappointed. If there was any link with Renshaw, Margaret Falconer could tell him nothing, and Blades thought it probably a waste of time asking about Jack Osgood but he did anyway, only to receive a derisory snort and a no.

'Just a couple of more questions,' he said, 'and then we'll be on our way, and I'm sorry we've had to ask you so much.'

Peacock interrupted at this point. 'Mrs Falconer, you must eat some of your own delicious cake. I insist. Did you make it yourself? And drink some of your lovely tea. That pot makes a really nice cup.'

'Yes. I did make the cake myself,' she said. 'There are still some things I can manage, even if I do have to take a seat in the middle of doing it.' Then she suppressed another sob. 'Fruitcake was Charlie's favourite.' As she stared into space, Blades could see that Peacock was regretting bringing up the subject of cake.

Blades decided the best thing was to make her concentrate on questions again. 'Did you notice any change in Miss Wright's behaviour or habits after her father's death?'

Mrs Falconer looked puzzled. 'Yes. She was in grief.'

'And what did she do to cope with that?'

'Her father was a demanding invalid and she couldn't go out much before his death, but she went out even less after he'd died. She did get better after going to that Spiritual church. I'm a firm believer in that as well. That Digby Russell's a treasure. He put me in touch with my son who was killed on the Somme. It was ever such a comfort to know he's all right where he is now. I can look forward to seeing him again when my own time comes. And Digby's a good-hearted soul. He came around to see Evelyn a lot, and it helped her.' Mrs Falconer looked more cheerful now. A wistful look had appeared on her face.

'You didn't think there was anything romantic in the relationship?'

She frowned, and Blades could tell he was trying her patience. 'I don't know what would put that into your head unless it's malicious gossip.'

'Did she spend much time away from the house latterly?'

'Anything I know about that I got from Charlie, and he said she was away at Leeds not that long ago for a few weeks. He said it would do her good to have a nice holiday.'

'Was she away at any other time?'

'I think he said she was away a couple of other times. We assumed she was in Leeds then too. I couldn't tell you what she did when she was on her travels but I'm sure it was all proper. You wouldn't expect anything else of Miss Wright.'

It had been confirmed Evelyn was away on more than one occasion, but Margaret Falconer obviously knew nothing that would shed light on this. Blades had learned nothing at all from this interview. Tactfully, and politely, he and Peacock withdrew.

'We'll try to find this man who killed your husband. We'll put our best efforts into it. You have my word for that.'

# CHAPTER TWENTY-NINE

From the dining room window, Katy, Mary, and Janet had a grandstand view of the murder scene as the police worked on it. The lawn was designed to show the beds to their best advantage from that angle, and they had clear sight of the measuring, the photographing, the talking and nodding, and the shaking of heads and striding about, then the parleying again that Blades and Peacock occupied themselves with round the centre bed with the luxuriant purple lupins and the unfortunate corpse. They had also observed with curiosity as the doctor had poked and prodded at it and noted things down in his notebook. Then they had seen him and Blades standing with their serious looks as they spoke and listened to each other, that mysterious but energetic jabber noiseless to the watchers. They had seen the doctor leave and Blades and Peacock walk into the gardener's cottage, leaving a corpse under a tarpaulin in a flower bed with a constable standing guard beside it, while a crowd of other large constables crawled around the gardens on their hands and knees searching for anything that might resemble a clue, and looking from the distance not unlike, to Katy's mind, overgrown schoolboys dressed up in fancy dress and looking for a toffee that they had dropped.

'Poor Charlie,' Katy said. 'He wasn't a bad old stick.'

'He looked fierce,' Mary said, 'but he was gentle as a lamb.'

Janet nodded and muttered something they could not quite make out, but which sounded sympathetic.

'Who would do that to him?' Katy said.

'Do you think it was the same person who did in Miss Wright?' Mary asked.

'You wouldn't think there would be two murderers around here,' Katy replied. 'I hope not, anyway.'

'Do you think he saw something on the night Miss Wright died?'

'He must have done.'

They both stood and contemplated the scene.

'Why wouldn't he just tell the police?' Katy said. 'He liked Miss Wright. She'd been good to him. She gave him time to nurse his wife. There's not many places that would take on a gardener who needed to spend hours away from his gardening to fuss round his better half.'

'Was he afraid of someone?' Mary wondered.

'If that's so, he was right to be. Look what they did to him.'

'You don't think he did tell the police what he knew?'

'And the murderer didn't know that or what?'

'Maybe.'

'The police will have their theories,' Janet said, 'and they'll be better than ours. We're just making things up.'

'Still, it could have been something he saw,' Mary said.

'How could he have seen anything?' Janet said, 'With him in his cottage that evening and well away from the house?'

'He could have looked out of the window,' Mary said.

'He couldn't see through the house walls to see what was going on in that drawing room, could he?'

'Could he have seen someone going into the house?' Katy said.

'That could be,' Janet admitted.

'He couldn't have been having arguments with someone in the pub?' Mary said. 'My Dad does that. Comes home with a black eye sometimes, or worse. He can't hold a drink my mother says, but that doesn't stop him tossing it back.'

'Charlie doesn't go out to the pub,' Katy said, then stopped before correcting herself. 'Didn't go out to the pub. I still can't believe he's dead. He was standing in the kitchen with a basket of peas this morning.'

'He's definitely dead,' Janet said.

'You don't think the murderer will turn on us, do you?' Mary said.

There was a mocking look on Katy's face as she turned to Mary. 'You think he's got the blood lust? You think he'll be desperate to cut the throat of a juicy young girl now?'

'You're horrible sometimes, do you know that?'

'Stop bickering,' Janet said.

'I don't know if I want to stay here,' Mary said. 'Someone's murdered two people in this house. Who knows what they'll do next.'

'It bears thought,' Janet said. 'We don't even know if we'll have jobs in a few months' time.'

'Do you think I should be looking around for something?' Mary said.

'I didn't say that,' Janet replied. 'We need all the servants we have to keep this place in order over the next few months till we find out what's what.'

'I know what you mean, Mary,' Katy said. 'How do we know what's going to happen? If Charlie was murdered because of what he saw or even just because of something someone thought he saw, maybe they could think we noticed something too.'

The two girls and Janet looked at each other.

'You could just go home,' Katy said to Mary.

'I was glad enough to get away,' she replied. 'I don't want to go back. But it might be sensible and it's what my mother wants me to do.'

'That's what she said when she was round to see you?' Janet said.

'Yes. For the meantime, she said. And that was after Miss Wright's murder. There have been two now. There's no way she'll want me to stay. Won't your mother want you to go home too, Katy? Will you go?'

'How could she do that?' Janet said. 'She's an orphan.'

Mary stared at Katy. 'Are you? But I thought you said–'

Katy looked into the middle distance and said nothing.

'What have you been telling her?' Janet asked Katy, who blushed and stayed silent. Then Janet turned to Mary. 'Katy's just the same as me. She was brought up in an orphanage and trained to service there. This is her life, same as it's mine. She won't be going anywhere, and neither will I.'

At that moment, Katy spoke. 'Look,' she said. 'They're coming out.' Janet and Mary looked in the direction Katy was now pointing, where they saw Blades and Peacock leaving the gardener's cottage and striding towards the house.

'They'll be coming to ask us something next,' Katy said.

'It won't do them any good,' Mary said. 'None of us knows anything.'

'It won't stop them asking,' Janet said.

Then, after a long pause, Katy added, 'No. None of us knows anything.'

# CHAPTER THIRTY

'You've been watching everything,' Blades said as he strode into the dining room and approached them.

Three heads turned and gazed at him with guilty expressions.

'You're quite right,' he said. 'Anyone would be curious. And alarmed. I hope you're not too distressed. There will be one policeman around here at least over the next few days guarding that crime scene till we've decided there's no more to be gained from it. That'll put any murderer off.' Then Blades paused to give himself time to consider his words, which gave them more weight. 'Though you do have to consider seriously whether there is a reason any of you might be at continuing risk. If you know anything about either crime you need to tell us. This isn't a casual murderer. He killed both Evelyn Wright and Charlie Falconer for a reason.'

Both Blades and Peacock did study them, but there was nothing to be read on any of the servants' faces except bewilderment.

'Though if he has nothing to fear from any of you, you probably have nothing to fear from him.'

As there was still no answer from the women, Blades started making his questions more exact. 'The doctor said he thought Charlie Falconer had been dead for about two hours. Did any of you see or hear anything suspicious or unusual about that time.'

'About two o'clock?' Janet said.

'Approximately,' Blades replied.

'I was in my office,' Janet said.

'I was in the kitchen,' Katy said.

'And I was dusting upstairs about then,' Mary said.

'So, all three of you were in completely different areas of the house?' Blades said.

'You mean none of us has an alibi?' Katy said.

'You think one of us could have done that?' Mary asked. 'You don't think that of us?'

Blades gave them all as unreadable a look as possible. 'We always consider every possibility,' he said.

Peacock smiled at Mary and his voice took on a kind tone. 'However unlikely.'

Mary smiled back and blushed.

'Did you hear any movement in the house?' Blades asked. As there was no reply, he continued. 'Is it possible any of you could have left the house without the others knowing?'

'No,' Janet said quickly, followed by Katy. 'I would have heard the servants' door opening from where I was.'

'And the front door?'

Katy thought. 'Right enough. Someone could have gone in or out that way.'

'And you?' Blades asked Mary. 'Could you have heard anyone?'

'They could have been going in and out all afternoon and I wouldn't have heard a thing from where I was,' Mary said. 'Except I'm sure none of us did go out.'

'You know that for certain? How?' Blades asked.

'None of us had a reason and I know what everyone's like,' Mary said. 'And none of us would have gone out there to murder anyone.'

'From the housekeeping office I would have heard anyone go in and out,' Janet said.

'Good,' Blades said. 'I'm glad to hear that. Now I'm going to ask you all to wait till Sergeant Peacock has the chance to see you all individually to take your statements.'

But Blades was disappointed because he'd learned nothing.

# CHAPTER THIRTY-ONE

The interview Blades had with his Chief Constable was tricky.

'Two dead so far. Three last time. And we still don't know who was causing murderous mayhem on Birtleby beach. How many more bodies do you think there will be before you find this killer, if you do?'

Blades took that to be a rhetorical question and said nothing, just sat there opposite his superior and wondered where he was going with this. Blades was not in the habit of squirming and did not like the way he was shifting about on that hard seat, apparently designed to be as uncomfortable as possible.

Archie Moffat, Chief Constable of Yorkshire, banged his impressive fist on his desk and gave Blades a long perusal from particularly steely grey eyes. He did have a large head, Blades thought as it loomed in his direction from the huge body swelling out of Moffat's uniform. Blades knew that in his youth Moffat had been athletic, a keen rugby player no less, but the impressive physique of the prop forward can run to fat without continued exercise and working behind an administrative desk did not provide a lot. But although there was a softness to Moffat's body that would not have been there when he was a young man, his sheer size did lend him a formidable appearance, and Blades found it easier not to meet Moffat's eyes when he was in a mood such as the one he was now in.

'Walker was demoted the last time. I defended you for a reason I now forget.'

He tapped a finger before continuing.

'That was the worst advertisement for this force in memory and I had the embarrassment of it being on my watch. "Chaotic police force bungles again" was one of the least damaging headlines. I only just kept my job over that and God knows why you kept yours. I must have gone soft in the head.'

Blades opened his mouth to reply but then thought better of it. Perhaps this storm would blow itself out, though he doubted if it would happen quickly.

'Why didn't I call in Scotland Yard this time? After the last time I'd no faith in them but it would have been easier to defend if I had.'

Blades thought he might venture a reply now. 'I was flattered that you didn't, sir, and grateful for the support you gave me over the last case.'

'I should hope so too,' Moffat thundered.

Now he twirled his moustache.

'My argument was that our force is now at full complement for the first time since the beginning of the war and that we have the men and the competence to deal with this. I was forlornly hoping for a feather in my cap.'

And you're also saving the force some money, was Blades' thought. 'We may catch him yet,' he said.

'It's your job. You're supposed to.'

'I'm sure we will, sir.'

Moffat looked down at the reports on the desk in front of him, and proceeded to leaf through them, grunting at regular intervals.

'You've dismissed three suspects so far.'

'Pulteney was hanged, sir, before we realised he hadn't done it. We might have had egg on our faces but it was worse for him, so we have to be sure. We can't make a mistake like that this time.'

'Obviously not. But have you lost your nerve? Some people would think so. Why not Osgood?'

'We can't place him anywhere near the crime and his fingerprints don't match. There's no motive either. He gained nothing financially from Evelyn Wright's death and he's rich anyway as his bank statements show.'

'And why not Renshaw?'

'He's guilty of fraud but not, we think, murder. He has a record for embezzlement and, when we checked with his bank, we discovered he's in debt now. He's been betting with bookies again, which is why he's been selling share certificates to a mine in Argentina, fraudulent ones, and we're arresting him for it. But we've had no choice but to dismiss him from the murder inquiries.'

'Why? He's a good fit. He was involved with Evelyn Wright, he's been placed in Birtleby with her on at least one occasion, and you may not have placed him there at the time of the murder but he has no alibi for it.'

'His fingerprints don't match those on the murder weapon.'

Moffat glared at him as he pushed away the files in front of him and pondered before eventually snapping, 'Would you be prepared to arrest anyone over this one or not?'

'Of course, sir, but we need to observe due caution.'

'We have to stop these crimes. How do we know there won't be more deaths?'

'We don't,' Blades admitted.

'And what about this Digby character?'

'Inconveniently for us, he has the wrong fingerprints too.'

'A charlatan. I call him that because he acts out séances for a living. And he was a young man hanging about an older woman to see what he could get. Shell-shocked. Reliably documented as mentally unstable. And you dismissed him as a suspect too.'

'The mistakes we made the last time made us murderers. I don't want to repeat that.'

'That's a bit of a statement. Would it be easier if I took you off the case and did call in Scotland Yard?'

'No, sir.'

'I'm not sure about you, Blades. Your confidence is shot as far as I can see.'

'I'm confident, sir.'

'Or you may have gone soft. I don't think it would be difficult for our murderer to talk his way out of things if he's faced with you. I can see what these men are, smarm experts. If they can charm and chatter their way round women to get what they want, they might talk rings round you.'

'I wouldn't be so sure of that, sir. I see these men for what they are. I just have to make sure I don't see them as worse than they are.'

Moffat tapped his obese finger again if less energetically but, though some of the tension may have been raged out of him, he still showed concern.

'How many women are there in that household?'

'Three. There were four, but Margaret Falconer has gone to live with her sister. She'll need support at a time like this and, in any case, she's arthritic. She needs care. The three servants are still living in the house. That's Janet the housekeeper, Katy the kitchen maid and Mary the chambermaid.'

'There's still a murderer at large there. You'll need to provide protection. I know it will mean taking men off inquiries, but we can't have any more women murdered.'

'As you say, sir.'

'And what is the course of the rest of your inquiries?'

'With reports still coming in, there is a lot to follow up and confirm. And men are assigned to ask around for witnesses. We've also put out another press statement. More witnesses may come forward. The crime scene is still being searched for evidence.'

'Cover every angle on this. I don't want hit and miss policing, do you understand?'

'Yes, sir.'

# CHAPTER THIRTY-TWO

It was the end of the day and Blades had planned to go home by now but could not stop himself pacing about the grounds of Elmwood Hall, and Peacock had stayed with him. The body had been taken away but there was still a constable guarding the crime scene. There was also a constable at both the back and front of the house so that, if the killer returned, there was protection for the servants, but Blades still turned over possibilities in his mind. Would it be possible to gain entrance to the house unseen from anywhere? The windows had been checked and they were securely fastened. He had walked about and checked till he had even annoyed himself with this, though Peacock remained customarily restrained. Blades stopped his striding beside the centre bed where Charlie Falconer had met his end.

'If Charlie saw something on the night of the murder, where would he have seen it from?' Blades asked, continuing to sweep his eyes around him.

'Charlie said he finished work at about half five, so it wouldn't have been from the grounds.'

'Unless he went out for some reason?'

'Which his wife says he didn't.'

'Which she was unaware of. If he'd seen something from a window, he might have gone out to investigate. Otherwise, what is visible from the cottage windows?'

Blades and Peacock walked over to the cottage, then turned and looked back towards the house.

'Those trees and that hedge block any view of the road,' Blades said. 'They also block any sight of the drive up to the house but not the area directly in front of the main door or the servants' entrance, so that he could have spotted someone entering or leaving.'

'If that's what happened why did he keep quiet about it?'

'Someone he knew and felt loyalty to? One of the other servants?' Blades said.

'It could have been,' Peacock agreed, 'though he'd only been here a year, which is not long to build up quite that much loyalty.' Then Peacock frowned. 'Or not.'

'This is the first indication it could have been someone in the house.'

'Though it might not be something he saw. He might have heard someone say something,' Peacock said. 'It might have been someone who had some hold over him, which is why he didn't speak to us about it. He might have been in debt or someone might have known something about him.'

'Or perhaps he secretly disliked Miss Wright and was glad?'

'That's not how he came across when we interviewed him.'

Blades and Peacock stared at the house, each now deep in his own thoughts. Then Blades spoke. 'You were out at the Front. What was it like?'

'The war? Why do you want to know about that, sir?'

'Everybody who didn't go has questions about it.'

'Believe me, you were better off here. And you were doing an essential job. There would have been anarchy if no one had stayed behind to do any policing.'

'How did you get through it?'

'Get through it? That's a good question. I didn't expect to with all those bullets and shells flying around. I was lucky.'

'A bullet hits you or it doesn't. I know. But how did you will yourself to go on?'

Peacock looked in Blades' direction. 'There wasn't any choice.'

'I suppose that would be right. All the same, I find you difficult in some ways.'

'You do, sir? I'm sorry about that. I do my best with my work.'

'That's not what I mean. You're difficult to understand. You're self-contained. You get on with your job no matter what, just do it competently without letting anything upset you, yet we deal with genuinely difficult things. Things always upset me.'

'Things get to me too, sir. I just don't see the point in moaning about them or letting myself be beaten. You asked me what it was like at the Front. It was hell, but you got on with the situation in hand. You didn't let yourself dwell on emotional things. It didn't help.'

'I often wonder how I'd have managed out there.'

'You'd have done all right, sir. You get on with things too.'

'I wonder. This case is getting to me.'

'We'll solve it, sir. We'll get him.'

'You don't every time. We've no glass to see into men's souls and tell us who did the murder and who did not. Those Ridges murders got to me. I haven't recovered from them, and here we are with another brutal murderer and no idea of who he is this time either.'

'We'll get him, sir. Just believe it. Then we might.'

'Maybe.'

# CHAPTER THIRTY-THREE

Jean was staring at Blades as she waited for a reply. It was comfortable in their sitting room, their seats angled towards each other in front of the Victorian tile fireplace with its dark wood mantle. It was after their evening meal and, with their son Alex out at his scout movement, there was time to talk. Blades sipped tea from a china cup as his brows furrowed in thought. Jean had just asked him again if he would consider her father's offer.

This was familiar territory to Blades: how to react to the earnest importuning of Jean. He knew she had probably saved his life before by persuading him not to join up, or rescued him from permanent injury, both of which had been the lot of so many men at the Front, though, if it had been his duty to accept either fate, he did not think he would have minded. He did have to convince himself he had no regrets about yielding to Jean. At the time, she and her mother had been devastated by the death of Jean's brother at the Somme; such had been Jean's distress she'd been unable to concentrate on anything, and he'd been worried about her. Jean's father, wanting to look out for his daughter, had put in his arguments too.

Policing had been valuable work during the war and he hadn't regretted playing his part in it. With so many men away, there were fewer to protect people's homes and there had been the usual level of crime. Someone had to deal with it and provide an impression that there was something there to be feared if the law was broken, the police, the courts, and the prison system. Normal life had to continue despite the chaos on the continent. He had done his duty but part of him had yearned to be at the Front with the others. He knew how much men were needed out there.

Now Jean was trying to persuade him to do something else he did not want to do: accept her father's offer. Blades realised that it was a good one. He wanted his son-in-law to take on the management of one of his stores, of which he had four, all of which were prosperous, and it was work Blades might relish. There was another factor too. Jean's brother Tom had been the only son, and both Jean and her father thought it would be good to keep the business in the family, which Blades could understand, but again it felt like he was being asked to take the coward's way out.

It was Jean who broke the silence. 'I'm tired of seeing you worn down by that job. You work so hard and I'm sure you do well, but I don't like to see you suffer the way you do.'

'Someone has to do it,' Blades replied. 'It might as well be me as someone else.'

'It wasn't your fault that murderer wasn't caught. It was that Scotland Yard detective, Walker. But the press crucified you too. I hated seeing your name dragged through the mud.'

'It's the job. We're in the public eye. There's nothing can be done about that, and we have to get results.'

'But it's happening again. I want you out of it. It's not your fault there's a murderer around. Let them blame someone else. You don't have to stay on in that job. You can do something else. Why don't you?'

'We might catch him this time.'

'Or you might not. And he might go on killing.'

'I'm not sure he's that kind of killer. There's a specific set of circumstances here. We just have to explore them.'

'I don't want you pilloried like that again. Taking a job with my father is sensible. Do you see that?'

Blades didn't see how he could persuade Jean to think otherwise. Nor did he see how he could cave in to avoid all this pressure. He wondered what Peacock would do faced with this conversation. Peacock was a man he admired more the longer he worked with him. Blades would have liked to know if he would have coped at the Front as well as Peacock. Could he have done as much? Could he do this now? Could he ignore his alarm and anxiety and get to the end of this investigation?

'You don't understand what you're asking me to do,' he said to Jean. 'I might have ducked out of one war, but this is another one and it's mine.'

'I don't know what you mean,' Jean said.

'There's a battle going on between this murderer and me. And I need to win it.'

Jean looked at him mystified.

# CHAPTER THIRTY-FOUR

The policies of the editor of the Leeds Chronicle were totally different from those of the editor of the Birtleby Times. As far as he was concerned, murder cases were a golden opportunity to provide lurid headlines, and the one he gave to this article was designed to draw as much attention as possible.

## SPINSTER'S DOUBLE LIFE LEADS TO HER MURDER

*As has been reported already, Miss Evelyn Wright, spinster of Birtleby and heiress to the Wright biscuit manufacturing fortune was found murdered on Friday, July the 27th, in her mansion at Evans Gardens in Birtleby. What is now known is that Miss Wright was leading a double life. Though a well-respected figure in her own community, she had taken to spending time in Leeds where she dressed much younger than her years, even provocatively.*

## HOW MANY MEN FRIENDS DID SHE HAVE?

*There she led the life of the scarlet woman, meeting up with men, one of them a man by the name of Jack Osgood, with whom maids confirm she shared her bed in the hotel. Another of the young men hovering around her has been named as Peter Renshaw, a man with a criminal record for embezzlement. Questions have also been asked about her relationship with Digby Russell the Spiritualist Minister, who apparently was rarely away from her house in Birtleby. It might be speculated that one of these men might have committed the murder, and all have been questioned by the police, but all have also been dismissed as none have fingerprints which match those on the poker found beside the body, and which was the murder weapon. Who did those prints belong to? Some other young man she'd been seeing?*

## WHO COMMITTED THE SECOND MURDER?

*Miss Wright's gardener, Mr Charles Falconer, has since been found murdered in her grounds – on Thursday, 9 August. The police state that someone must have crept up behind him as he went about his duties, and hit him with a gardening shovel, which was left lying nearby. Again, there are no witnesses to the murder and, in this case, no suspects, though the police consider the two murders to be connected. Had Charlie Falconer seen something on the night of the first murder? If so, he might have said something to someone. If anyone has any information, the Birtleby police would like them to get in touch.*
*The police would like anyone with information of any person in the vicinity of either murder to come forward. Also, does anyone know of any other young men she might have been seeing? If so, information about those would be welcome.*

## A DIFFERENT WOMAN SINCE HER FATHER DIED

*Miss Wright had always lodged with her father, being his sole companion after the death of her mother, and she also cared for him through a long illness. Being from one of the wealthiest and most prominent families in Birtleby, Miss Wright at one time attempted to provide leadership in the community and was prominent in her Methodist Church, and on charity committees, but, since her father's death, she had been believed to have become reclusive apart from supportive visits from a Spiritualist Minister. It has thus been a surprise in the local community to discover Miss Wright's conduct elsewhere. No one can believe her behaviour in Leeds, and it is believed it led to her demise.*

Blades was disappointed with the article, which he thought unfair on Miss Wright, and he did not care for the practice of destroying someone's reputation for the sake of selling newspapers. He had viewed the body and thought enough harm had been done to her. It could be difficult to feel sorry for the rich, but, as far as Blades could see, Miss Wright's wealthy background had not helped her. With that possessive father of hers, she had little life to herself when he was alive so perhaps it was no surprise that she threw over the traces energetically once he had gone, and Blades wondered what was wrong with that. She was not being unfaithful to a husband, and surely it was natural to snatch at a bit of life while she still had the chance? This took him back yet again to the murders on the Ridges. Those victims were all young women. The lives single women led. Until joining the police he had not realised how difficult they could be. He hoped that scandal sheet would at least bring out more witnesses.

# CHAPTER THIRTY-FIVE

Constable Flockhart had found the duty of hanging around Elmwood Hall, on the off-chance a murderer might turn up, boring. It had been reduced to a single-person duty but it was twelve hours on before he was relieved and was able to enjoy his twelve hours off, and why did he have to draw the midnight to mid-day shift?

As he stood outside the front door in a conspicuous position, he reflected they were unlikely to catch any murderer with him standing there. As soon as a would-be-killer saw him they would be off, though that was the intention, crime prevention not criminal apprehension. The women inside were worthy of the attention, chatty, friendly and likeable every one of them, but he was surprised that so much care was being taken with servants. Perhaps he was too cynical. In any case, he could have done without this extra duty. He did not like standing about outside at night-time. There were a lot of hours involved in policing and, he reflected, the least his efforts ought to earn was a good night's sleep.

An owl hooted further off, and something scampered unseen in the bushes, the usual night-time sounds of wildlife, but there was not much hint of human activity.

The occasional car rumbled past, headlights blazing its presence, and there was one carriage. A couple announced themselves with voluminous chatter as they strolled unworriedly past the front gate, feet clattering on cobbles.

Constable Flockhart continued to stride the area of his post. As usual, at the beginning of a shift, every noise or hint of movement was noted, but then, as routine dulled the senses, his mind wandered, mostly to football. League tables had been a passion of Flockhart's since football had resumed after the war. He had missed it. It was the most important symbol of the return to normality for him. He thought of the match on Saturday last, which his shifts had allowed him to see. A couple of goals had been the result of howlers but there had been a wonderful one. Armstrong in full flight on the wing had been a sight to see as he had stopped suddenly then moved inside his man to direct a hard, pacey cross in the direction of Harry Watson who had powered a header down and past the outstretched keeper. A moment to savour, and he reminded himself of it now, the cheers of the crowd, the sudden uplift of spirit at the success of a goal after all those minutes of effort, running and tackling and passing and sweating, then the release of all that tension in the celebration of scoring. Men competing against each other and proving themselves with a football made far more sense to Flockhart than battling it out with bullets.

But a flicker of light from inside the house brought him back to the moment. That light had come from where? The third floor? The servants' quarters. It was silent now with no sign of movement, but he supposed someone must have been restless in the night and needed to pay a visit to the toilet. Constable Flockhart waited and watched. He ought to check the doors. The front one looked secure but he should check the back door and the servants' entrance. Making great use of his flashlight, he walked to the side and checked there, tugging at the handle. He was relieved to find the door still locked. He then walked round the back of the house and tried the rear entrance which was also as it should be. He continued to shine his flashlight around, but there was no sign of anyone, so he made his way back round to the front. There he looked up at the servants' floor again and stared at it for some time. He did not like the thought of someone sneaking past him and murdering one of these women. He decided to check inside as well. He unlocked the front door, opened it, and walked in. As the house was dark, he kept his flashlight on. He picked his way along the hall and up the stairs.

He was impressed by the quietness of the house. The only noises were from outside. He swept his eyes around him as he moved forward. Once on the servants' floor he could hear the noise of quiet snoring from one of the rooms and was glad to note that at least one person was having a peaceful night, but as he crept along the passage there was a crash behind him, then the movement of feet. He cursed himself for swinging his flashlight round too late.

A door opened, and he turned towards it to see Janet standing there in her nightgown with a bewildered expression on her face, a poker she must have taken from the fireplace in her room held in one hand.

'What are you doing?' she bellowed at Constable Flockhart.

Flockhart dropped his light, and it went out. He bent down retrieved it with a fumble then switched it on again. 'What are you doing wandering around here in the middle of the night?' she asked him again.

'I'm on duty,' he said. 'It's my job.'

'It's not your job to scare the living daylights out of me,' Janet replied.

The doors to the other two servant bedrooms had opened by now and Katy and Mary stood there, clutching nightgowns around them and gazing at him.

'What's going on?' Mary asked.

'Have you caught someone?' Katy asked Flockhart.

'Did you hear any noises?' Flockhart said.

'I heard someone blundering about,' Janet replied, 'and when I opened my door, I found you standing there.'

'Did you not hear something crash?' Flockhart asked.

'I did,' Mary said. 'That's what woke me. Then I heard Janet and then you.'

'Where did that crash happen?' Flockhart said, flashing his light about. It came to a stop at an upturned occasional table and a plant pot on its side. Flockhart stared at it. 'Now I didn't do that. Were any of you out of your rooms?'

'Not me,' Janet said.

'Nor me,' Mary added as did Katy.

'So who did that?' Flockhart asked.

All four of them stared at the pot. 'Someone must have come in,' Katy said.

'They're not still in the house?' Mary said.

'You were supposed to be protecting us.' Janet pointed her finger at him, her voice raised. 'Where were you?'

'Where I was supposed to be,' Flockhart replied, 'standing guard outside the front door.'

'And you let someone walk past you,' Janet said.

Flockhart gave her a hard look. 'Obviously not,' he said.

'So how did someone get in?' Janet's eyes glared at Flockhart.

'They could still be in the house,' Mary said.

'I'll check that,' Flockhart said.

'Don't leave us by ourselves,' Mary said.

So Flockhart found himself followed closely by all three as he prowled around, checking for any intruder. He did not mind this as it made it possible to do both duties at once, protect them and unmask the person who had broken into the house. It was Janet who found the open window on the ground floor on their tour of that area.

'They're nowhere in the house,' Flockhart said. 'We've checked everywhere.'

'They must have gone out that way as well,' Janet said.
'So it seems,' Flockhart replied.
'Thank God for that,' Mary said.
'You're telling me,' Katy agreed.

# CHAPTER THIRTY-SIX

'An intruder in the night?' Blades asked Flockhart.

It was now the next morning, and daylight at least made the scene look more cheerful.

'He gained entry here,' Flockhart said as they stood in the hallway looking at the open casement window. Blades strode over to it and peered out at an area of lawn and a flowerbed. He turned back to Flockhart.

'Has anyone touched the window?' he said. Seeing Flockhart hesitate, he said, 'Was it you?'

'I didn't touch it,' Flockhart said. 'I don't think anyone did.'

'We'll check it for prints as a matter of course,' Blades said. 'We have everyone else's but we'll need yours as well. What was it that first alerted you to this?'

'I was at my post.' Blades noticed how clear Flockhart was making this though he had not thought to doubt him. 'Then I noticed a flicker of a light in the servants' quarters. It's not out of the ordinary to need to find the washroom in the middle of the night and at first, I thought that was what it was. But I investigated, and as I was doing that there was a thump and I wasn't able to see who'd caused the noise. Then one of the doors opened and Jane challenged me with her poker.'

'Good job you weren't the prowler, Flockhart. Might have been your early demise.'

'Then the other two bedroom doors opened and Mary and Katy turned up. I found the source of the thud. Someone had knocked over a plant pot.'

'We'll have to have a look at that,' Blades said.

'And then when we searched everywhere, we found the open window.'

'Careless of them to leave it open behind them,' Peacock said.

'But lucky for us,' Blades said. 'You've done well, Flockhart. Someone was up to mischief all right, but you've kept the women safe. Peacock, you'll have to dust this window for fingerprints and photograph it. Have a look outside as well and see if you can find footprints to take plaster casts of. And we'd better have a look at this overturned plant pot too. Show us to it, Flockhart.'

This Flockhart did, and Blades ruminated on it. Flockhart then took him on a guided tour of the whole house and Blades examined this corner and that, tut-tutting as he did so, though he wasn't always entirely clear about what himself. This was a puzzle. He found himself staring at fire irons as he walked past and wondered why he was becoming fascinated by them. When they had finished, he said, 'We'll interview the servants, and we'll have a good look at that weapon Janet was wielding in your direction. It'll be the one from the fireplace in her room. Good job it wasn't one from the drawing room. That would have finished you off quickly.'

Flockhart snorted. He did not seem sure how to take that.

# CHAPTER THIRTY-SEVEN

'My mother says I'm definitely not safe here,' Mary said to Janet as she stood with her coat laid out on the bag beside her, all ready to leave. 'It's not only Miss Wright who was murdered, so was Charlie, and you wouldn't have thought anyone would want to do him in, so who's next? There's a maniac around, that's what she says. And she could be right. Who was that prowling around in the middle of the night? Not that she's happy at the thought of having me back. She was pleased to be rid of me, one less mouth to feed, and I was sending money home. And my sister Jessie will be furious. She'll have to share her room with me again.'

Janet had little to say in reply. 'Your mother knows best. You pay attention to her.' But she was wondering at the duties that would be left undone. She supposed Katy would take on Mary's jobs in addition to her own. Katy would manage as there would be less to do with the only rooms in use being those of the servants, and kitchen duties were light as Janet only had Katy and herself to cook for now. Why did they continue doing things anyway? Janet mused, and why did she still bark endlessly at Katy? There was no Miss Wright to appease and her father was gone. Janet realised she was the one who had become the tartar. She was so disciplined by years of habit to supervise the household to the standards that the Wrights set that she was incapable of doing anything else now. It might keep her going through this, she supposed.

Katy was livid with Mary. 'Don't go,' she said. 'Pay no attention to your mother. I don't want to have to whiten that front step again or black-lead the kitchen range. I thought I was finished with all that.'

'My mother doesn't want me working in the kind of place this is,' Mary continued. 'What that Miss Wright was up to. Who'd have thought it?' Then, with all the wisdom of her fourteen years on her face, Mary said, 'Think of the reputation I could get if I kept on working here. I wonder why you don't all leave.'

We might have to, Janet thought. We don't know whether that Andrew Wright will want to keep us on or not.

'You don't want to worry about what old gossips say,' Katy said with a superior scowl.

But Mary moaned on. 'And my mother was ever so pleased when I got this job,' she said, 'because it was supposed to be such a grand household and look how it's turned out.'

'I'll give you a good reference,' Janet said. 'You haven't been here long, but you'll get a suitable place somewhere. You're young and healthy.'

When the bell at the servants' door rang, Mary picked up her bag and trudged off in answer. Her mother was there as arranged, with a virtuous expression above her cheap and worn coat, and she took Mary's hand in hers as they trotted off.

Lunch in the servants' hall, which Janet's kitchen doubled as, was never a grand occasion but was even less so with only two of them. Janet ladled pea and ham soup into bowls as she and Katy sat and supped in gloomy silence.

Eventually, Katy asked, 'Did you know anything about what Miss Wright was up to in Leeds?'

'Not a thing,' Janet said. 'That's not something the mistress would share with the likes of us.'

'And there's me not allowed to have a boy round to pick me up on my night off. I had to meet up with anybody somewhere else.'

'It's true. She didn't encourage followers. She's let girls go for that.'

'And that's what she got up to.' Katy didn't notice that her voice was becoming louder the more she moaned. 'And her so goody-goody and behaving as if she was some sort of saint. She thought she could get away with that just because she had money. Not that it did her any good. Look how she ended up.' They both ate more soup. Katy contemplated each mouthful as if expecting wisdom to be found in it. 'Who do you think did her in?' Katy said.

'Never trust a man,' Janet said, 'and you can take your pick of three here.'

'I never liked the look of that Digby. He was a ghoul.'

'A lot of people do like him,' Janet said. 'They say being put in touch with a loved one's a blessing.'

Katy thought about this. 'You said it was a con to get money out of people.'

'I was talking to Cavendish our grocer. He lost his son at the Front, and his wife swears by Digby Russell. She says her son spoke to her through him, and says it was definitely his voice, and how could Digby put on the voice of someone he'd never even met?'

'You said you still think he could have done the murder?'

'I don't know what to think,' Janet replied. 'The whole thing's a mystery. But it wouldn't surprise me. Nothing would.'

'And Charlie Falconer! The paper must be right. He must have known something. Did you hear anything on the night Miss Evelyn was done in?'

'I was down in the basement. Anything could have been going on up there and I wouldn't have heard it. And Charlie never spoke about anything to do with the murder with me. I don't know what he knew.'

'Nor me.' Katy was waving her spoon about above her plate while eating none of the soup. When she became aware of Janet staring, she put it down.

'Eat some of that instead of worrying on so,' Janet said. 'It's good soup.'

'Sorry,' Katy said, and picked the spoon up again to help herself to some. Then she said, 'Did you ever see anyone like that Peter Renshaw around here?'

'No.'

'Nor me. And I wouldn't mind seeing what that Jack Osgood looks like. He sounds a bit of a card.'

'Wouldn't touch him with a barge pole.'

'Nor me.' But there was something wistful in the way Katy said this.

Janet thought back to the household and the tasks that would have to be assigned. She and Katy were still working for someone, Evelyn's brother. Would he keep the household on or not? He had his own in Harrogate and Janet wondered how attached he was to it. Still, after a lifetime of service, doing household tasks was a habit and it was easier not to break it.

# CHAPTER THIRTY-EIGHT

Information usually came from a variety of people, some of whom Blades had put behind bars himself, and others he knew ought to have been put in jail if proof had been more forthcoming. These were the grafters seeking payment for information they had or did not have, but who could be helpful with their inventions. Blades did also meet law-abiding people earnestly trying to help, unremarkable men or women who looked around nervously as they sat in front of him and behaved towards a police officer with the utmost respect. He also met his share of pure fantasists leading lonely lives, and who seemed in need of company. Some witnesses were poorly dressed and in need of a wash; others had obviously made the effort to dress respectably for a police station. Few were anything like the pair Blades now saw in front of him. They were a fashionable-looking couple, he with his jaunty cravat, and she with her outré cloche hat, and they sat in front of Blades in his office. He was tapping a brass-topped cane absent-mindedly, while she dabbed a lace handkerchief to an eye before returning it to a silk purse. Blades felt underdressed for his own police station.

'You say you've information for us?' he said.

It was the gentleman who spoke. 'I'm Arnold Hopkins,' he said, 'and this is my fiancée, Miss Eleanor Benson.'

'Pleased to meet you,' Blades replied. 'I'm Inspector Blades.'

Then he waited to see what Arnold had to say.

'Eleanor's parents live on the same street that Miss Wright lived on.' He paused as if choosing words with difficulty, though what he went on to say was unremarkable. 'We were returning from an outing in town and I was seeing Eleanor to her home.' But after that, he was at a loss for words.

'What day was this, sir?'

'It was the day of Evelyn Wright's murder, July the 26th.'

'That's interesting. And about what time was it?'

'I don't know. About eight?'

'Was there something that you saw?'

'We thought nothing of it at the time. There wasn't anything to notice. Though I remember it. It was a young man in a fashionable style walking up a fashionable street. Nothing you would remark on. What did strike me was how cheerful he looked, as if he'd just come into some good fortune or thought he was about to. When he tipped his hat to you in the passing, he did it so affably. I doffed mine in return and Eleanor nodded to him, and we bid each other good day. And why should I remember that? We were discussing our wedding. I thought it should be next June, but Eleanor thought it should be earlier, which is important to us; so why was my mind drawn so far away from that? The point is I noticed him, and he fits the description in the paper. After he'd passed us, I looked back at him, and he was turning into Miss Wright's drive. And there was something so cocky in the way he did that. And I wondered what a young man like him could want with Miss Wright. She's a neighbour of Eleanor's and we know all about her, dowdy old thing that she was. And here's a young man in his twenties, fit-looking, handsome, and with such a spring in his elegant step as he walked up her drive to see her. And that's it. I suppose that's why I remember it. It wasn't that he was so remarkable in himself, but he was so incongruous there.'

Blades had seated himself further forward in his chair as he listened to each word and took in every nuance. 'Would you describe him in more detail, please?' he asked.

Now Eleanor spoke. 'He was about average height.'

'Tallish, but not as tall as you,' Arnold said.

'Fair-haired,' Eleanor added, 'and with a short, neatly cut fair beard as the newspaper said.'

'That's right.'

'Oh he did have blue eyes, a very pale blue,' Eleanor said, 'and a charming manner. He'd a taking smile if it helps.'

Oh yes, Blades thought. It would have helped. A charmer. Just the sort Evelyn fell for.

'Did he speak at all?' Blades asked.

'He didn't say much,' Arnold replied.

'Good evening. Lovely weather, isn't it?' added Eleanor.

'Something like that.'

'Did you notice his accent?'

'Not from round here. A southern accent, I'd say,' Arnold said.

'Cockney.'

'Maybe.'

'Visiting Miss Wright?' Blades asked.

'I did wonder about that at the time,' Eleanor said.

'And how was he dressed?' Blades asked.

'In a navy-blue coat,' Eleanor said.

'With a navy-blue felt hat,' Archie added.

'And a natty cane.'

'Ebony with a silver handle and tip, and he swished it forward as he walked, tapping the pavement.' Arnold demonstrated the movement of the cane with his own as he spoke.

'And this was what time again?' Blades was beginning to think he couldn't believe his luck.

'About eight on the evening the paper said Miss Wright was murdered,' Arnold said.

'Which was another reason you remarked on him?'

'After reading the paper, yes.'

'But you didn't see fit to come forward before now. Why?'

Arnold and Eleanor looked at each other for support. Arnold eventually said, 'Disbelief? Just reading about the murder was incredible. The thought we'd seen anything that might matter – it didn't occur. And you don't like, you know, the thought of being involved in something of that sort.'

Eleanor squeezed Arnold's hand as he simpered at Inspector Blades.

'You've come forward now, and it's useful. Thank you, sir. And was he someone you'd ever seen about the place before?'

'No,' Arnold replied. They looked at each other again, then almost in unison, said, 'No' again.

'So you don't know who he might have been?'

'Unless he was a relative,' Eleanor said. 'I didn't know she had that many, but you don't know every single one people have, do you?'

'No, indeed,' Blades replied.

'He might have been some sort of distant relation,' Eleanor said.

'Though later,' Arnold added, 'after reading what the newspapers said about Evelyn, we thought he might just have been one of her young men. Not that we'd have thought that of Evelyn. She seemed a bit dried up if anything.'

'It's surprising how much life people have about them. You'd never guess it sometimes,' Blades said. 'Have you seen him since?'

They agreed that they hadn't.

'So, this wasn't something you remarked on at the time, but, in retrospect, you thought it might be of interest to us?'

'Yes,' Arnold said as Eleanor nodded vigorously.

'Which it is. Thank you.'

And as he had gained from them everything there was, he closed the interview. 'I'll have you make a statement to my sergeant if you don't mind.'

'Of course,' they said.

# CHAPTER THIRTY-NINE

Though he hadn't quite lost his perennial trace of doubt, Blades was starting to feel something akin to excitement. Could they be closing in on their man? There was one thing for sure, with the adrenalin surging through him, he would be giving this everything. They had a major missing piece where Peter Renshaw was concerned. He'd been placed at the scene on the day of the murder, and at the time of it. It was unfortunate that, once again, fingerprints didn't match, but, even if he did end up being dismissed as a suspect, he'd been at the scene. He could have noticed something.

Blades decided to interview Renshaw at the police station, so he sent a constable to fetch him from his showroom. He was reluctant to come at first, but on being told he could come voluntarily or under arrest, he agreed. It caused consternation in the showroom as had been intended. The constable told Blades that the receptionist had given him a knowing look, and the other salesmen had looked pleased too. Blades suspected Peter Renshaw, for all his charm, was not popular at his place of work. This didn't surprise Blades who thought that behind Renshaw's smile lay an arrogant and insensitive individual. When

Renshaw arrived at the station, he was shown to the interview room.

As Blades had made Renshaw wait, he was surprised to see the casualness of Renshaw's slouch in the chair when he entered. He and Peacock seated themselves opposite him as Peacock took out his notebook and made a show of positioning his pencil ready to start.

Blades had found Renshaw so continually annoying and shifty it would give him pleasure to find proof against him, so he decided to put some pressure on. 'You've already been told of the case we're assembling against you for fraud,' he said. 'You're now here to be formally interviewed as a prelude to a possible charge of murder, that of Evelyn Wright of Elmwood Hall, Evans Gardens, Birtleby. What you say may be taken down and used as evidence against you. You are entitled to a solicitor if you wish one.'

In reply to this, Renshaw cast a lordly eye at Blades and said nothing. It was then that Blades realised the extent of Renshaw's arrogance. Blades would have expected some sign of nervousness, but Renshaw still looked as if he considered he had nothing to fear from the likes of Blades and Peacock.

'Then we'll continue,' Blades said, though he didn't, and instead treated Renshaw to some arrogance in return as he stared at him in silence and studied him further. When Blades did speak, he did so slowly and not without menace.

'In a previous interview, you said you did not know Miss Wright. Do you still maintain that?'

Renshaw replied immediately and with an irritated rush of words. 'Yes. You've got the wrong man. Again. It's quite a reputation you're building up, Inspector Blades.'

Blades did not allow the riposte to fluster him. 'We've already had you in a line-up and you were identified then as someone who had visited Evelyn Wright in Birtleby and who had been seen going about with her elsewhere.'

'I've no idea where you get your witnesses from. They're very imaginative. Or are they just short-sighted?'

'We've unearthed another couple of them, sir. You were seen walking up Miss Wright's drive on the evening of the murder.'

'Was this before or after I'd been seen walking around in the gardens there with Miss Wright?'

'At half past seven on the evening of the murder.'

'I was at home that night working on some paperwork for the office,' Renshaw said.

'For which you have no witnesses.'

'And you've found another pair of short-sighted witnesses, ones who don't know which day it is.'

'Really, sir?'

'I'm writing every reply down,' Peacock said.

'You can deny as much as you like, sir, but we have a few witnesses now who can place you with Evelyn, and at her house, and that even on the night of the murder. It's called a weight of evidence. One witness might be doubted but an accumulation of accounts usually does convince a jury.'

'But you've told me I was trying to sell Miss Wright mining shares. Why would I kill her if I was trying to do that? Dead people are not good customers,' Renshaw said.

'Perhaps you could tell me, sir.'

'I can't.'

'The evidence we have is enough to charge you with murder, sir. And then the prosecuting counsel makes his persuasive case and the jury decides. And you sound guilty to me.'

'And me,' Peacock replied.

Which was all bluff as Blades knew. Once you took the fingerprints into account – again, Blades thought – there was no case to answer. But he did not mention this to Renshaw. It was a comfort to Blades when Renshaw started chewing his thumbnail.

Then Renshaw spoke. 'All right, I did know Evelyn. And I was there that night.'

Then Blades could feel the excitement returning. 'So why deny it?' he asked him.

'Someone's going to hang for that, and I don't want it to be me.' Peacock continued writing as Blades just gazed at Renshaw. 'As I say,' he continued. 'I did go over that night. I thought I might convince her to buy shares, but I didn't go into the house. She already had a visitor. There was a car in the drive. When I saw that I went away again. A wasted trip. But never mind. They happen.'

Blades considered that credible before he remembered another thing Moffat had said. Renshaw was a smarm merchant used to charming and talking his way past people. Was he playing on Blades to talk his way out of this?

'And what did the car look like, sir?'

Then Renshaw described the car.

# CHAPTER FORTY

Blades did not like where he was with this case. He'd still found no suspect who was an exact fit. Perhaps if he reviewed the evidence and the exhibits? It was always something that had to be done. And he did.

First, he studied the photographs of the crime scene. Though he had looked at them so often they were inscribed indelibly in his mind, he still had the feeling he had missed something but, if he had, he did not find it. He reviewed the statements of all relevant witnesses and lamented the paucity of conclusive information. They had proved that Peter Renshaw had been at Elmwood Hall on the night of the murder but that did not establish that he murdered her because of the invisible man who they knew had left fingerprints on the murder weapon. Blades read the medical report on the body again. Two blows to the head: one to kill her, the second to be sure, but there was no record of who wielded the poker in the description of her cause of death. Blades smoked a few cigarettes and drank a few cups of tea as he went through the reports and statements again and again and looked at everything and anything in the evidence bag. Then he picked up some items, put them in his own bag, and found Peacock, who had been writing up a report.

'Let's have another look at that murder scene,' Blades said.

They traipsed back to Elmwood Hall. After Janet had given them entrance, Blades and Peacock strode up to the drawing room, where Blades stood and perused the scene, Peacock beside him.

'Let's review what happened,' Blades said. Then he strode over to a chair. 'Evelyn Wright was seated here with her book when Digby Russell came in. She put that down, poured him some port and they chatted.' Now Blades walked over to the fire. 'Digby stood here, and at some point, Evelyn got up and moved towards him, leaving her glass on the side-table, half empty. When they had finished their conversation, Digby's glass was completely empty and he left it on the mantlepiece. There was a mild disagreement, a simple faux pas according to Digby, and then Digby left, leaving Miss Wright – according to Digby's evidence – hale and hearty.'

'I follow you,' Peacock said, though he did look to Blades as if he was wondering where this was leading.

'But when Miss Wright is next seen she is found lying dead on the carpet in front of the fire. Possibly the disagreement was greater than Digby says, and he lost his temper and murdered her, using as his weapon the poker from that stand by the fire.' At that point, Blades took out the poker from its exhibit bag and displayed it to Peacock.

'Or possibly he is telling the truth. In which case, it could have been Renshaw who visited Miss Wright and did the deed. We've established he was in the vicinity around the time of the murder. Similarly, with Jack Osgood. He knew Miss Wright – intimately – and we know he knew his way to her house, and we can place him in Birtleby itself, and Renshaw says a car like his was there on the night of the murder, which we might try to establish. But why can we place none of these extremely sinister men in the murder room at the time Miss Wright was murdered?' Blades now flourished the poker.

'Because the fingerprints on this do not match the prints of any of them. Every strand in the investigation, every interview with a suspect breaks down at that point.' Then he shifted his eyes from Peacock whose reactions he had been watching and turned them to the poker which was still aloft in his hand. 'So, I suggest we examine this particularly important piece of evidence again.'

'Or find who the fingerprints do belong to?' Peacock said.

'Possibly. But one thing at a time. We need Mary in here.'

When he summoned Janet and asked her to fetch Mary, she told him that Mary was no longer working there and had gone to stay with her mother. But Blades had an idea in his head now which he did not wish to relinquish, and that was to bring Mary face to face with that poker. After finding out the address from Janet, he and Peacock drove over to it.

# CHAPTER FORTY-ONE

It was a sandstone tenement block with nothing to distinguish it from any other apart from the individual weathering on the sandstone. It was one of those built to house industrial workers, including employees from the Wright Biscuit Factory, Blades supposed. Such blocks had been built notoriously cheaply and were crammed full of people. There were even some who just lived on the stair in such buildings. Blades and Peacock trudged upwards to the top floor where they knew Mary's family lived. The stone steps had a deep downturn in the middle from the wear of so many feet. The walls were decorated with pale green tile, broken and cracked in many places. But Blades noticed that the stairway was clean. The people living there must take their communal tasks seriously, he thought. When they reached the top landing, they perused the different doors and Peacock rapped on one with its knocker.

It was Mary who opened the door to them just as she had at the Wright household. She no longer wore her maid's uniform but a rather fatigued floral print that looked as if it might have been handed down from her mother.

'Good evening, sir,' Mary said, with a questioning lift to her voice.

Blades gave her an encouraging smile. 'Sorry to bother you again, Mary, but you were very helpful and there are one or two more questions we'd like to ask you if we may.'

'Of course, sir,' Mary said and showed them in.

The room she took them into seemed to double both as kitchen and living room, with some weary-looking seats in front of the kitchen range. The other furniture in the room consisted of a table and chairs, and there were some shelves covered with a variety of crockery and pans. A woman whom Blades took to be Mary's mother was seated by the range and she stood up to meet them.

'This is Inspector Blades,' Mary said.

'And Sergeant Peacock,' Peacock added.

'My Mary's been through enough,' Mrs Cunningham said. 'Why have you come to see her again? I won't stand for her being harassed.'

Mary's mother was a spry lady of not much body weight but with commanding eyes and an edge to her voice that suggested someone who might be used to struggling to get by but who had more than enough determination to make sure not only that she did, but also that her daughter did. And Blades was not the first large man to find himself quailing before her.

'Indeed,' Blades said. 'You're right. We do need to treat her properly. And we will.'

But Mrs Cunningham must have been awaiting her opportunity to voice her feelings to the police. 'You've no idea how much she's been upset by all this. I had to take her away from that house because of the effect it was having on her. She's only a girl, and you have to be careful with girls.'

Blades' appeasing smile was the most winning he could manage. 'You're right,' he said – again. 'But your daughter could be an important witness.'

'To what?' Mary doesn't know anything and she's a good girl. She's done nothing wrong. She's fourteen. I should have been there when you were questioning her before. You'd no right.'

Blades considered this. 'She was working away from home as an adult. And there was another adult present, Janet Farrell.'

'I ought to have been there all the same. I'm her mother. I'm not leaving her alone with you this time. If you want to question her, you do so in front of me.'

'As you wish.' Now Blades signalled to Peacock. 'Bring out the fire iron set from Miss Wright's and lay it on that table.' Peacock took them out from a leather bag. Then Blades took the poker from the evidence bag that he carried and laid it beside the other irons. 'Now Mary, I want you to look at these.'

'Yes, sir.' Mary came over to the table and peered at them. 'Is that the poker that killed her?'

'It is.'

She gasped. 'And is that the blood still on it? That makes you shudder. Poor Miss Wright. She was a proper lady. It's dreadful to think she's been killed.'

'You're right. It is.' Blades showed patience, but he wanted his questions answered. 'Now the fire irons. You must have cleaned these often enough.'

'I cleaned the fire brasses all right, sir, faithfully, till they shone bright as anything, and every day.'

'Look at them more carefully. Is there anything you notice about them?'

Mary ran her eyes over every single one, slowly, trying not to miss any detail, sighed, looked up at Blades, then perused them again. A puzzled look appeared in her face.

'That can't be right.'

'What?' Blades said. Peacock's and Mary's eyes stared at the poker, as did her mother's. Blades continued to study Mary's face.

'The brass on that poker's different,' she said. 'It's not as dark a yellow.' There was a surprised note in her voice and her eyes stared. 'The pattern's the same. If you didn't look at the brasses altogether, there's no way you would notice. Now that's funny.' Her eyes continued to run over the tongs, the shovel, the brush, and the poker. 'They're very alike but that poker's newer. It's as if it was bought at a different time.'

'You cleaned them every day,' Blades said. 'And it's the first time you've noticed that?'

'Yes,' Mary said, as she continued to stare. 'Now why wouldn't I see that?' Blades, not wanting to put words in her mouth, waited. Then the words rushed from Mary. 'It's a different poker. That's not the one I cleaned every day. It couldn't have been. I would have noticed. Now, why is that a different poker?'

'You're quite sure?' Blades said.

Mary considered the poker again.

'As sure as I'm standing here,' she said.

'You'd swear to that in court?'

'Court? I don't want to go to court.'

'What's this about a court?' her mother said. 'Mary's done nothing wrong.'

'As a witness only,' Blades said. 'And it might not be required. But that is how definite you are?'

Mary stood looking between her mother and Blades, unsure about how to respond.

'Go on, Mary,' her mother said. 'Just tell him the truth.'

'It's not the same poker. I'm sure of that. But how did a different poker get there?'

'That's for us to establish,' Blades said.

'Janet won't be happy.'

'What do you mean?'

'She was particular about the brasses and that's an odd set now. She had me polish those brasses over and over till I got it right sometimes. And the thing is, with them being used in the fire, they did pick up stains, and you didn't get rid of them easily. But there was no excuse. She's demanding. Even with the mistress sometimes.'

'The mistress?' Blades said.

'Liked to know well in advance what meals were required so she could be all organized. She's a brilliant cook. You should taste her soufflé. But she's pernickety.'

'With the mistress?' Blades asked again.

Mary caught her breath. 'Oh, the mistress' word is law. Or was. But Janet did question her sometimes. I don't know how she had the nerve. I wouldn't myself. It was because she's worked in that house thirty-five years as she's always saying, I suppose. She even had a bit of a row with her not long ago.'

'Did you hear any of it?'

'It was only a few words, still they were going at it.'

'And the words were?'

'It was just as I was walking in with a tray and then they turned and looked at me and they seemed to remember themselves. I didn't really catch what it was about, but I did hear the mistress saying, "I'll thank you not to question that."'

'Did you talk about this with Janet later?'

'Oh, yes, sir. Janet said the mistress had been discussing the next week's meals with her and she was wanting changes from the usual, which I think Janet took to be a slight. But there you are. Miss Wright pays the wage and if she goes off your suet dumplings, you'd better cook something else, I suppose. Not that there would be anything wrong with Janet's suet dumplings. I couldn't believe the food in that house when I first saw it.'

'I couldn't credit it either when she told me about it,' Mary's mother said. 'I was jealous of what Mary was getting to eat, never mind what she said her mistress was being served up.'

'So, Miss Wright definitely said, "I'll thank you not to question that"?' Blades said.

'Janet had told her the new menu would take far longer than usual, as new menus do.'

'So, a disagreement about something minor?'

'Not that you'd have thought it anything minor the way Janet reacted to it. She was seething.'

This Blades wondered about. Why all the emotion and tension over that?

# CHAPTER FORTY-TWO

The new poker must have come from somewhere, and Thompson's, the ironmongers in the centre of Birtleby, seemed the sensible place to start looking. Or it could have come from a house close by, or further away, or anywhere at all. But if it had come from Thompson's that would make things simpler, so Blades and Peacock paid it a visit. There were other ironmongers in Birtleby, but Blades knew from the bills he had seen in Miss Wright's desk that the Wright household dealt with Thompson's.

The shop windows held a cornucopia of daily items, tin bread bins, buckets, and a variety of white china milk jugs. A selection of baskets hung from a rope suspended from above the front door so that you were compelled to view these items for sale as you entered. There was also a display of tools in the window on your left as you went in. But there was no sign of fire irons anywhere in what could be seen displayed outside the shop.

When they entered, they saw a man in brown overalls standing behind the centre counter serving a customer. Behind him was an array of wooden, labelled drawers, holding screws, nails, washers, and rawlplugs amongst other things. When Blades looked to the right, behind a row of brass coal scuttles, he saw an assortment of fire irons, some in brass, some of iron painted black and some in plain iron. Blades and Peacock walked over and perused these. Peacock picked up one poker and studied it before dismissing it. When the shopkeeper had stopped serving his customer, Blades approached him.

He was a middle-aged man, almost completely bald but pink-skinned and healthy-looking. He was a fleshy man obviously used to a comfortable life, who had an easy-going and ready smile for customers, which he now used as he addressed Blades. As the name above the shop was Edward Thompson and this man looked like the owner, Blades assumed he addressed Edward Thompson himself.

'How can I help you, sir?'

Blades gave him a polite smile in return. Then Blades put the evidence bag on the counter in front of the man, extracted the poker, and said, 'I'm looking for a matching set of fire irons for this.' As he did this, he produced his card. 'It's a police matter.'

Thompson stared at the poker. The traces of blood were still on it, but he didn't allow himself to be discomfited. 'Possibly through the back,' he said, then turned and walked into his back-shop. He came out with a couple of pieces from a set and laid them on the counter to compare. Then he said, 'When you look at them side by side, they're nothing like each other, are they?' He turned and took those irons back through, before coming back with some more, which he also placed on the counter beside it. 'That's a match,' he said.

Blades and Peacock stared, then a grin appeared on both faces at the same time. 'Have you sold any others like this recently?' Blades asked.

The shopkeeper stroked his moustache as he pondered. 'I can check my books, but the answer will be no. This is the only set like this in the shop, it's still here, and we haven't stocked this type before.'

This was disappointing, and Blades and Peacock said nothing at first before Peacock spoke. 'Do you sell individual pokers similar to that?'

'Close to it anyway.' Then Thompson opened a drawer below the counter and pulled out one that, on careful scrutiny, did match the poker from the evidence bag not only in design, but equally importantly, in the tone of the brass.

Blades struggled to control his excitement. There might be a solution to the murder here if he could grasp it.

'Has anyone bought one of these lately?' Peacock asked.

'We've sold a few in the last month,' the shopkeeper replied, 'but I don't keep a record of everyone we sell a poker to.'

But Peacock didn't give up easily.

'You do business with Elmwood Hall, don't you?'

'The Wright place?'

'That's the one.'

'Is this to do with the Wright murder?' Thompson said, and gave Peacock a look that held a surprising amount of tension. 'Yes. Janet often comes in here. She's the housekeeper there.'

'She didn't buy one of these pokers, did she?' Peacock said.

Apparently not liking the possible significance of his reply, the shopkeeper paused before making it. 'Janet? Oh, yes. She did buy one of those.'

'Can you say when?' Blades asked.

The shopkeeper hesitated again. 'A few weeks ago, which would've been before Miss Wright's murder. You're not suggesting Janet did it, are you?'

'I'm not suggesting anything,' Blades replied. 'I'm establishing facts.' But the shopkeeper was right. That was where Blades' thoughts were tending, not that he could understand why Janet would do anything like that, or how switching pokers fitted in the murder scenario, but it would bear pondering.

Then, as they turned to go, Peacock asked one final question. 'And do you remember anything about the other people you sold that poker to?'

# CHAPTER FORTY-THREE

The drive back gave Blades time for thought. He was considering that if they were succeeding in establishing the murder weapon with the mysterious fingerprints was not used to kill Evelyn Wright but had been switched with the one that had, then the obvious line of thought was that there might not be any reason to dismiss Renshaw from the investigation. After all, he was there, and he had a record. But what was the motive? Could it have been frustration because he could not sell his mining shares to Evelyn and he was desperate for the money? Had she been insulting about it? Blades supposed it was possible if it did not entirely convince him. Or Jack Osgood? Had he done it? The prints on the poker did not clear him anymore either. Renshaw had described a car at the scene as one similar to Osgood's, though similar was not enough when Osgood had so many witnesses providing him with an alibi. And was testimony from Renshaw reliable? This took Blades back to considering Digby and he wondered whether he ought to have dismissed him as a suspect. He was beginning to feel he had been faced with one conundrum after another which he may have thought he had worked out but that he could make neither head nor tail of now.

His mind was running to Janet as well. Anybody linked to that house had always been theoretically a suspect because of their connection to it, but there had been nothing else that had pointed to her. Then the thread of Blades' investigations, the trail of the poker whose fingerprints did not fit, did lead to questioning her.

Blades thought of what his mother had said of the lives of servants. She had enjoyed her life in service though she had been glad of the chance to leave her position of cook in a grand household because marriage had given her children and a family life. She was glad of the skills she had learned in the kitchen, and the work ethic she had acquired in service; she still kept an immaculate range, and cooked meals that made the mouth water. But then Blades' mother always had a positive attitude to life. Even when their cottage had been flooded, she had rallied quickly from the initial despondency and said it was an opportunity, not a disaster, a chance to make their home better than it had been before. She had held the same position in service that Janet did, and Blades couldn't imagine his mother committing murder. Though they were different people with different personalities. If it was possible Janet had committed these murders, what led up to this?

Blades thought of what he knew about Janet. She was an orphan who'd been brought up and educated for service. That must have been a difficult childhood. He supposed she would have relied on the other girls for companionship and support. The staff at orphanages varied, he knew. No doubt they meant well, but it was employment for them, not the natural relationship of parent to child. And some of them may have overdone discipline. But she had a sister, and at the same orphanage, he supposed. That must have helped. Wait though. What was that story Janet had told? Something about when her sister had died? Janet had not been able to go to her when she was dying because of Mr Wright. That was reason enough for her to hate the Wrights, he supposed. Janet's sister had been the only family she had, and with the circumstances of their upbringing, they must have had a close bond. But thinking of her murdering Evelyn Wright because of that stretched the imagination.

Then another thought occurred to Blades. Hadn't Janet also directed them to Digby Russell when he had been under suspicion? In retrospect, he supposed that could have been a ploy to distract attention from her. What was it she had said? A charming man but smarmy. And she had said more than that. She had said he was a queer fish and she did not think much of him herself. Oh yes. And that was it. 'He talks to the dead if you like and gets everyone to believe him.' And she had said something about his eyes. Digby had a light-hearted way with him, but his eyes were different. She had made him sound sinister. Not that she had said that much, Blades supposed, though none of it had helped their suspect. But none of it had been damning and Blades did not suppose it pointed the finger at Janet now.

Peacock was driving with his usual placid concentration. Blades was often pleased with the backdrop of calm that Peacock provided.

'So, it looks as if Janet could have bought the murder weapon,' Blades said.

'It looks likely,' Peacock replied.

'Although as the ironmonger had sold a few exactly the same from that drawer, it could have been purchased by someone else.'

'Do you think one of our other suspects purchased one?' Peacock asked.

'If that's the case, where's the one Janet bought? We'll have a search of the Wright house. The simplest explanation is usually the correct one but I really can't think why Janet would have murdered Evelyn Wright.'

'One of the purchasers Thompson described sounded like Jack Osgood.'

'I'd wondered about that,' Blades replied, 'and Renshaw described his car but there's still the matter of his alibi.'

'We know he's committed one murder and got away with it, so he's capable of thinking he can commit another one without being caught.'

'Are we sure he murdered his mother?' Blades asked.

'You've met him. Did he show any feelings at all about his mother's death?'

'None. I berated him for it.'

'He's callous,' Peacock said, 'just the type to have done that murder and this one too.'

'A cold-hearted, self-centred bastard whooping it up on his mother's money without a trace of conscience about how he acquired it?'

'That's him.' Peacock nodded.

'So he'd be perfectly capable of murdering Evelyn for her money. Except, as we've said before, he didn't get any from her death.'

'There is that,' Peacock agreed.

Blades considered. 'Maybe something went wrong, and he realised his charm wasn't working so he killed her out of spite? He does have a certain self-conceit.'

'I'd check Edward Thompson's fingerprints against the ones on the poker we had down as the murder weapon,' Peacock said.

'I didn't have him as a suspect.'

'I don't either, but they could still be his prints. He could have sold the poker to the murderer and handled it then.'

'Which was a nice ruse on someone's part to confuse us. Which it did. But we don't have Thompson's prints.'

'Which is why I filched one of his pokers.' There was a mischievous smile on Peacock's face as he said this.

'That's theft, Sergeant Peacock.'

'In a good cause, and I'll find a way of returning it.'

Blades was looking at him askance but not without some hidden admiration. 'You could have just bought one,' he said. 'Or we could have asked him for his prints.' Then Blades became lost in thought and said nothing, just staring ahead of him.

Peacock glanced across. 'Is everything all right, sir?'

That had to be it. Though I will need proof; it was odd, he thought. As a detective, he spent so long hunting down the truth but when he found it, it wasn't something he'd slowly and agonizingly constructed out of half-hearted clues and suggestions. It was something that had found him. It ripped open the curtain it hid behind all by itself.

# CHAPTER FORTY-FOUR

Mary was back at Elmwood Hall and she had not taken long to return. Perhaps she had never really wanted to leave. She had timed her arrival well for their break, but she knew the times of those. Katy had been about to finish whitening the front steps and was thinking about going through to the kitchen to put the kettle on for mid-morning tea. She had been smelling scones for a while, as they had been baked that morning by Janet.

'There's no getting rid of you, is there?' Katy said. 'Don't you have a position yet?'

'No such luck,' Mary said.

'It's not supposed to be difficult. Big houses are supposed to be crying out for help. Are you making any effort or are you having a holiday?'

'I'm happy to have a bit of time to myself, but I'd like a position. I'm in the way in our house. My sister was happy as Larry on her own after I left. The problem is the reputation this place has. As soon as they hear where you worked that's the end of it. Elmwood Hall's got a name as bad as a brothel. Maybe they're afraid I'll seduce the lord and master, and he should be so lucky. Or they don't want

195

somebody turning up in their house to murder me, or me murdering them more like.'

'But your mum's glad to see you back?' Katy said. 'She's the one who took you away.'

'I don't think she expected to be stuck with me.'

'It used to be a feather in your cap working at Elmwood Hall,' Katy said. 'Or so Janet says. Now the police keep asking if there were any other young men Miss Wright might have been seeing.'

'Who'd have thought Miss Wright would be carrying on like that the age she was?' Mary looked amused at the thought.

'And who'd have thought any young man would have gone within a mile of her?' Katy agreed. 'Love is blind.'

'Love of money in her case. Are they any closer to catching the man who killed her?' Mary said.

'They ask lots of different questions, but they don't tell us anything,' Katy said.

'What questions?' Mary asked.

Katy looked back at her. 'They've fairly been going on about that poker.'

'The one that shouldn't have been there?' Mary said.

'That'll be the one,' Katy replied.

'I don't understand that,' Mary said. 'Why kill her with a different poker?'

'You've got me.'

'Here, have you thought of going to the police yourself?'

'About what?'

'You know, what you said.'

Katy stared back at her. 'That's nothing. I'd just be adding to the talk.'

'Maybe.'

Janet's voice, older and harsher, now butted in. 'What's nothing?' she said. Neither Mary nor Katy had seen or heard her coming out and they wondered how long she had been standing there. Katy's mouth was open as she looked at her and thought about what to reply.

As she could not think of anything else to say, she just said, 'Nothing.'

Janet glared at her. 'Then don't gossip about it,' she said.

The fact that Janet was annoyed worried Katy. It did not do to get on the wrong side of her, and that was what she had done.

'But you can come out with it to me,' Janet said. 'What was all that about?'

Katy did not elaborate, and Mary kept quiet too.

'Finish that step then,' Janet said. 'That's what you should have been doing instead of gossiping.'

Then she turned on her heel and started to go in, before turning and saying. 'Then you'd better come in for your mid-morning break. And you're welcome too, Mary.' And she managed to give her a welcoming smile. 'How are you keeping?'

'So-so,' Mary said.

'You're welcome to join us,' Janet said.

Mary followed at Janet's heels as she went indoors again. Katy finished off before joining them. She saw that plates with scones and butter and jam had been placed on the kitchen table. The butter would be bought, but the jam was Janet's own as well as the scones. Everything would be light and full of flavour, the preparation timed to perfection. Janet was as punctilious in her cooking as she was in supervising the work of other servants.

Janet poured tea into china cups and offered sugar and milk. It was a long day in service and both Katy and Janet knew to make the most of opportunities to put their feet up. Katy sliced her knife into her scone and started spreading butter.

'There's enough talk about this place these days without us making any more,' Janet said.

Katy cursed herself for not seeing Janet earlier.

'Aren't you jealous?' Mary asked Janet. 'It sounds as if old Miss Wright was having quite a time of it.'

'She disgraced herself.'

'Servants never have as much fun,' Mary said.

'She didn't want any scandal attaching itself to the place from servants,' Katy said. 'I'd have to sneak out to see boyfriends, and well away from here.'

'All my adult life I've been in service,' Janet said. 'I've worked my fingers to the bone. I didn't think I was doing it for a trollop.'

Katy and Mary's eyes met for a moment before they looked away again. Both avoided looking anywhere near Janet as they concentrated on sipping tea.

'I could have had a husband,' Janet said, then became lost in thought. To her discomfiture, a tear appeared in her eye before being wiped away.

Katy was surprised at such emotion from Janet and at the news. She couldn't imagine Janet with a man, but she replied, 'He'd have been glad to have you. Any man would die for your cooking.'

'You, young things,' Jane said. 'You think that Great War's the only war there's ever been, but there were plenty before it, the Boer War for one, even if it wasn't as big. You didn't know I had a beau who was killed in that, did you?'

Mary and Katy looked at her. Realising her mouth was open, Katy quickly shut it. 'He was a sergeant from Wales and a tall good-looking fellow; he was walking out with me before a bullet took him. So instead of marrying him, I did my work here and looked after the house for Miss Wright's father, and for Miss Wright, and that was my life.'

'That's sad,' Mary said.

'I didn't know,' Katy said.

'I don't think I'll stay in service,' Mary said. 'Not that I seem to be able to find another job in it. I want to get married and have kids. And servants never seem to manage that. There isn't any time for it.'

'He wanted to marry me before he went back out to South Africa,' Janet said, 'but we couldn't organize it in time. So I never knew my Dai.'

There was silence again. Katy wasn't used to such confidences from Janet, and Mary looked embarrassed.

Then Janet continued as if she hadn't just been discussing her own life. 'You won't get a job outside service,' Janet said.

'No? Why not?'

'Once you're in service you're in it for life. That's why. Another employer won't take you.'

'I don't believe that,' Mary said.

'You hear it over and over,' Janet said. 'Girls go applying for jobs and they're suitable, and the employer wants them but when he finds out they've been in service they change their minds.'

'But why?' Mary asked.

'We're the lowest of the low. Don't you know that? It provides us with a roof over our heads and keeps us off the streets but we're at someone else's beck and call all the time. We fetch their privies and clean their toilets and front steps and back steps and everything in between. And nobody respects us for that. Why should they?'

'But you're a skilled cook,' Katy said. 'Most people couldn't do what you do.'

'Which might impress anybody if I was doing it all for myself. But I'm a servant. I do all the menial work while my lords and mistresses lounge about.'

'What about the nobility of labour?' Katy replied.

'The dogma they give out in orphanages? Maybe. But most people see us as skivvies. And Miss Wright took our hard work and the freedom it gave her to act like a hussy.'

Katy looked at Janet. There was an intenseness in the way Janet spoke that Katy was wary of. Why did she find it frightening?

# CHAPTER FORTY-FIVE

When Constable Flockhart walked into the station, no one said anything at first. After all, what was unusual about a police constable walking into a police station? And Flockhart was his usual self after a shift, a bit weary but affable – a quick pleasantry on the way past the desk, obviously glad to see the back of duties till the next time like everybody else, just the end-of-duty report to write up and he was finished. He opened the door of the constables' office, pulled out a seat, and started writing.

Then Sergeant Ryan's face appeared round the door, followed by the rest of Sergeant Ryan as he strode up to where Flockhart was seated. 'So, what's up?' Ryan said.

Flockhart blinked as he looked up from his report. He gave Ryan a nervous smile. 'Glad the babysitting duties are over,' he said. 'They were boring.'

'Who said they were finished?'

Flockhart looked back at him. 'The message came through,' he said.

'What message?'

'The phone call?'

Ryan gave him a questioning look and waited for him to explain.

'It was Mary who told me,' Flockhart said. 'I was outside the front door when she came out all excited and talking nineteen to the dozen. She did get it right, didn't she? Said Janet had called her back as she was leaving, it was such good news. There had been a phone call, Janet said, and she started asking Mary if she didn't feel like coming back there to work, seeing there was no danger now and she couldn't get a position anywhere else. Very cheerful Mary was. She said she didn't think there was any way her mother would want her to come back but she'd think about it. She's been having nothing but fight after fight with her sister since she went home again, Mary says.'

'So, who was this message supposed to be from?'

Flockhart scratched his head. 'That Mary didn't know. It was Janet that passed it on to her.'

'I thought Mary left.'

'She came back for a visit,' Flockhart explained.

'I didn't think they would call off that watch yet,' Ryan said. 'There was that intruder you reported.'

'I thought about that,' Flockhart said. 'It was probably just one of them up in the night.'

'So why would they need a window open to get in?'

'I wondered about that too,' Flockhart said. 'But we've no proof anyone tried to go in that way. There were no marks on the ground outside. Someone probably forgot to shut it before going to bed.'

'You think?' Ryan replied.

Flockhart gaped back at him. He was feeling uneasy about this. But he hadn't done anything wrong. Had he?

'I'll check this with Inspector Blades,' Ryan said.

A few moments later, Ryan returned with both Blades and Peacock.

'You received a message you were to leave your guard duty at the Hall?' Blades said. Flockhart thought the look on his face unusually anxious.

'Yes, sir,' he replied but felt no confidence as he said this.

'Not from us, you didn't,' Blades said. And Flockhart thought he'd never seen Blades' face that pale before.

# CHAPTER FORTY-SIX

Couldn't Peacock drive any faster? Blades thought.

'Put your foot down, man,' he said.

'I am driving fast,' Peacock replied but pressed his foot further on the accelerator anyway. At the next bend, the wheels screeched, and the car seemed to be pulling against him as they rounded it. He thought for a moment it was going to skid and he would lose control, but then they were round that bend and racing on to the next.

'I hope we're on time,' Peacock said.

'So do I,' Blades replied. 'I didn't think it would come to this. I should have acted by now.'

'So which one is it?' Peacock asked. 'Who phoned up to draw Flockhart off?'

'Flockhart was told someone phoned up. He didn't say he'd heard any phone ringing. It's someone who was already there. It's Janet.'

'She's cleared the field to kill Katy?'

'Charlie Falconer can't have been the only one who spotted something. Some of the things Katy said. I should have got it earlier than I did.'

'Janet must know we'd suspect anyone who arranged for the police guard to be cancelled.'

'She's panicked. Faster man,' Blades bellowed. 'She won't hang about.' Peacock put his foot right down and the car roared faster. 'But get us there in one piece.' Peacock gripped the wheel harder but didn't let his pace slacken.

But he was still able to ask Blades more questions. 'So that attempt Flockhart reported was by someone inside the house?'

'Who made it look as if someone from outside came in.'

'But Janet?'

'I'd a blind spot for her too. And she's committed two murders. What's the easy way out of problems for her now?'

Peacock accelerated past a carriage, spooking the horses that were drawing it in the process, then, as he reached the next bend, he found himself swerving to avoid a car coming around it. Then they were there, in front of Elmwood Hall. Peacock braked. Blades opened his car door and ran towards the house.

# CHAPTER FORTY-SEVEN

Kate was packing, not that she had much to pack. She owned enough to put in one suitcase. Was this all her hours of work every day had earned her? A few changes of clothes? Yet she had liked it here. It had been the only home she had known apart from the orphanage, and it had seemed exciting after that. There had been so many wonders in this house to admire. But she was frightened now. And where was she going to go? As she folded her dresses and placed them in her suitcase, she pondered that. She had decided to leave, but what was there to go to? The streets that the orphanage had trained her to avoid? The orphanage? No. It would not have her back at her age. Maybe she could go and stay with Mary till she found somewhere, though she did not know what Mary's mother would say. She might understand, Katy supposed. She had thought Elmwood Hall too dangerous for Mary and, if it was, it was too dangerous for her too. In fact, it was particularly dangerous for her.

She thought back to the night of Miss Wright's murder. She had finished her tasks and gone upstairs which was where she should have stayed as she was tired enough, but she was restless and made the excuse to herself she wanted a glass of water from the kitchen. Had Janet seen her when she was returning from doing that? She had been walking back up the servants' stairs when she heard the door open and glanced down to see Janet coming in. Janet had been absorbed in her thoughts. That was obvious. Something was bothering her, something that made her mutter and stare as she advanced in from the door and took the downward stair to the basement. Katy had never seen Janet looking like that before. And, apart from her ghastly mood, what Katy noticed about her was the dirt on her shoes and on the long sweep of dress above her ankles.

How had she got her clothes that dirty? It was so unlike the immaculate Janet, but Katy had seen her clearly in the light from the gas mantle at the bottom of the stairs and there had been no mistake. She could only think of one explanation for this and that had only occurred to her when Mary had told her about the poker. Janet must have been getting rid of the first poker. Katy continued packing. It was surprising how absorbed you could become in that, particularly at such a moment. It was a fold she was concentrating on when there was a footstep behind her, and she didn't hear it.

She did hear the noise that Blades made as he rushed towards Janet, and was surprised, on turning around, to see him lunging for yet another poker in Janet's hand. Surprised, Janet whirled and aimed it at him but then his right hand was on hers and it was stronger so that the poker was wrenched away and thrown to the corner. Then Blades had her in an armlock and there was no escape.

# CHAPTER FORTY-EIGHT

'I'm glad you stopped me,' Janet was saying. 'I don't know what came over me. I liked Katy.' There was a simper on her face that Blades hadn't seen before. He was just glad she'd calmed down. She'd been beside herself for hours.

Blades was looking across at her now in the interview room. Peacock sat beside him, and a police constable stood on guard at the door. Blades reflected on the ways his attitude to Janet had changed. He had thought of her as an ageing, mild-mannered housekeeper, and he'd always respected those because it was a position his mother had held, so he'd treated Janet in a manner that was almost deference. Now he knew her as a double murderer and, as he prepared to ask his questions, he studied her with no sympathy.

'You're the sharp Inspector Blades,' Janet said with a hint of a sneer but one which did not stay on her face. 'Which is my problem. You are. You'll have it all worked out, won't you?'

Blades did not reply to this but gave her space to say whatever it was she was going to.

'I knew you would when I heard Mary and Katy say you knew about the poker. Once you'd got that, you were going to get everything else. I didn't know what to do after that. I regret attacking Katy,' she said.

Blades noticed that the emotions on Janet's face were real and he was glad at least she wasn't a cold-blooded killer.

'I shouldn't have done that,' she said. Then her hands pulled mindlessly at the hem of her sleeve as she seemed to forget about Blades and Peacock and her eyes became vacant. She was there somewhere inside herself, Blades supposed, working something out.

'And Charlie Falconer?'

'You'll know about that too,' she said as she attempted to repress a sob and failed. Then her body shook as her emotions overwhelmed her again and a moan rasped out of her. After a moment, she said, 'Poor Charlie. No. He didn't deserve that. He was a good man who looked after his wife well, even if he was unfaithful to her – with me. That was something you didn't know.' There was a gleam in her eye for a moment as she looked at Blades. 'I still have some life in me. That surprised you, didn't it?' She cackled – briefly. 'It surprised me after the downtrodden life I've led. And I was fond of him, but he couldn't be trusted after he found out what I'd done. You do see that, don't you? I had no choice.'

Blades said nothing. She would make her excuses, though she did not look as if she were convincing herself, and they wouldn't help her avoid her punishment, but Blades didn't mind listening if it helped confirm what he knew.

'He said he would keep my secret to the grave, so I took him at his word, not that he meant it in that way. He saw me on the night of the murder and I couldn't let that go. He could have told anyone at any time, couldn't he? And how could I have been expected to know that Charlie would see anything? Everyone knows he goes back to his cottage every night. I didn't know he spent any time looking out of the window.'

Then she pulled at the hem of her sleeve again as her eyes glazed for a few moments. 'I had to bury that poker because I couldn't let it be found in the house.' There was a strange plead in her face as she said that. 'Not that it was the best of hiding places. I was going to get rid of it properly when there was the chance, but Charlie saw me burying it and dug it up again, and then he knew what I'd done. But I didn't want to kill him. Why would I? He was a comfort to me.' Then she paused before adding, 'It's too easy the second time.'

'Why did you decide to do away with Katy?'

'I knew she'd got something worked out. And she did see me coming back in from burying the poker. I had hoped it didn't mean anything to her. But something did. And it had to be that.'

'Do you regret killing Evelyn Wright?' Blades asked.

Janet glared at him as she gathered her thoughts to answer. Her eyes were dark and she scowled as she spat out, 'She was nothing but a self-centred, heartless scrubber.'

'That's why you killed her?' Blades asked.

Janet looked daggers at him as he waited for her answer. She was struggling with strong emotions.

'I saw her in the garden with that Peter Renshaw,' she said. 'Him so much younger than her, and her with her hands all over him, shameless hussy that she was. And everybody thought she was such a virtuous person. Evelyn Wright was supposed to be such a grand lady and look at the way she behaved. And she had that Digby Russell all over her too. I couldn't take any more of that.'

Then Janet wrung her hands as she gave vent to a sob, which was followed by a few more. When she had calmed down, she continued. 'You don't understand,' she said. 'How could you? I lost my Dai over her. You don't know about that, do you? That was in the Boer War. Her mother was organizing a series of soirées for her, so she could meet a young man, and her mother said I could easily manage to wait till Dai was next back on leave before our wedding. It wouldn't make any difference to me. Then Dai was killed out there, wasn't he? I never knew any man properly till Charlie.' That was only the second time Janet had talked about Dai and she was surprised how much it helped.

'That was her mother. That wasn't her,' Blades said.

'It might as well have been,' Janet said. 'It was for her. Dai would have died anyway, which was no one's fault but the Boers, but that didn't change the way I felt. I wouldn't have known him for long and might have even been left with his child, but I'd have loved that child.'

'Feelings do overcome the reason at times,' Blades said, but there was no sympathy in his voice.

'It's not as if it's the only way they made me suffer.'

Blades watched the emotions at work on Janet's face, self-pity and anger most prominent, but he could see no remorse there.

'It wasn't Mr Wright who stopped me going to see my sister when she was dying. It was Miss Wright, selfish besom that she was. I had good reason to hate Evelyn Wright and not just her mother. But you didn't know that,' she said, and Blades could see the triumph on her face. 'I hid that from you. I wasn't giving the police a motive gift-wrapped.'

'We already do know,' Blades said. 'Katy told me.'

'She did?'

'Yes. I did come back and question her again.'

'I didn't know you'd talked about that with her. I suppose that's what started her mind working.' Then Janet said nothing for a few moments, though Blades could see her mind was whirring and she was struggling with anger now. 'Miss Evelyn was going to sell up this house and turn us all out, ungrateful besom that she was. It was that night she told me, after Digby had left, and she called me up to the drawing room to tidy up. I've worked for her for thirty-five years and she was going to turn me out on the streets. She was going to go to Leeds if you like and shack up with one of her young men no doubt. I don't know. I just snapped. After I'd time to think about it, I walked straight into the drawing room and killed her with the poker.'

'You snapped?' Blades said.

'Yes.'

'I don't believe it was that night Miss Wright told you she was selling up the house. You had a big argument with her earlier. I was told about that. That wasn't just about a change of menu. That was about a change of house. No. You didn't snap. There was the business of the switched pokers, remember? That extra poker had to be bought in advance. You planned this. You won't escape a hanging with that argument.'

'The business of the pokers?' Janet laughed for a moment, then stopped as a gash of anger appeared on her face. Then that disappeared and a gleam came back into her eye. 'That was smart, wasn't it? After I'd killed her with one poker, I hit her with another. I only had to hold it by the shaft that time. She was already dead and it left those lovely fingerprints on the handle of the 'murder weapon'. You were never going to track them down. And I made sure I wiped my own fingerprints off the shaft. The only problem was getting rid of the poker I'd hit her with. Poor Charlie. It was a pity. And he'd done well by me. He hid it well. You won't find that.'

'We have found it. He didn't hide it as cleverly as all that,' Blades said. 'It was painted black and put in the kitchen set of fire irons, which was why there was an extra poker in that set. Though perhaps he would have done something about that if you'd given him the chance to do it.'

'If you hadn't got rid of him as evidence,' Peacock said.

Janet thought for a moment. 'He might have done.' Then Janet's face brightened as she attempted to rally. 'But those fingerprints threw you off,' she said.

'They puzzled us,' Blades said, 'but, on the other hand, they protected the other suspects. Just as the prints on the murder weapon weren't yours, they didn't belong to them either. Most people would have wiped their fingerprints off the murder weapon and left it at that. If you'd done that, we might have decided we had Digby dead to rights and closed the case then.'

'I'll bet you never found out whose fingerprints they were, did you?'

'They belonged to Edward Thompson, the ironmonger in Birtley,' Blades replied.

Janet's face fell at this. 'All wrapped up then?' she said. 'Just as well. I should never have done any of it.' Her face was grim now as she stared ahead of her. Then she seemed to rally as she said, 'Miss Wright did deserve her end. I've never felt so good as I did after swinging that poker. That'll show you, I thought. The life she was leading. And the lives her servants led to help her do it. It was unfair. All the same, I wouldn't have done it if I hadn't seen her with that young man in the garden.'

Blades wondered at that. Why was there the need to blame someone else?

'After that, I couldn't help thinking: just how many more men has she got secreted away?' Janet looked at Peacock who'd been scribbling away trying to keep up with what she was saying. 'But you don't need to worry about getting all that right, sergeant. I'll write out my confession and sign it. I won't avoid the hangman's rope. You won't allow it. But I'm not ashamed of what I did.'

And Blades did not suppose she was, though he felt duly ashamed for her. He pondered the other things Janet had said. What was that one again? How many more men had Evelyn got secreted away? There was a thought. The mysterious car in Evelyn Wright's drive on the night of the murder hadn't been explained. As Renshaw described it, it could have been Jack Osgood's car. It was distinctive enough. But Blades still had not worked out how Osgood could have faked that alibi. Perhaps it was a car belonging to another young man of Evelyn Wright's. One thing was sure. If Evelyn Wright did have other young men in tow, it was a secret she took to her grave. Blades hoped it was a good one.

# CHAPTER FORTY-NINE

Blades was writing up his report on Janet when another report arrived. There had been a lot of reports to read on this case, some about witnesses coming forward, some about witnesses not coming forward but who could be traced, reports on fingerprints, the autopsy, the inquest, and some were even reports about reports, he supposed. They had cascaded and seemed uncountable and endless, yet he had thought he had come to the last of them. This one was from Dr Anderson, Digby's doctor at Craiglockhart, and Blades had been anxious about that at one point, the time when they had thought Digby must be their man.

This doctor was not shy about divulging confidential information; he seemed proud of the detailed report he gave. He did admit to having formed a very real liking for Digby which was why he had decided to be so forthcoming. The thought of Digby being a suspect in a murder inquiry he had thought horrendous, which was why he felt he had to do as much as he could to clear him.

When Digby had been referred to Craiglockhart, Dr Anderson had met a patient in an acute psychotic state due to his experiences in the trenches. This was not a violent man, but a man who could not cope with violence, and who abhorred it. Indeed, it was this that had led to his psychosis. He had been overwhelmed by an irrational sense of guilt at the role he had to play in the war. The fact he suffered from hallucinations confirmed the severity of the psychosis. Time and therapy, which had included, in his case, mock séances, had helped and, when he had left Craiglockhart, he had, to all intents and purposes, been cured, though a return to the Front was not recommended. The doctor understood that the Spiritualist church was prepared to help Digby find his feet again, and he considered this would be helpful. He could make no comment on actual communication with the dead, though it was not his place to say it was impossible when so many did believe in it. Digby seemed to believe the dead spoke through him, though the hallucinations had, as far as the doctor could see at the time, stopped, which would be consistent with the progress of psychoses. The doctor did not think the role of medium in the Spiritualist church would be harmful to either Digby or those who consulted him. And who was he to say it did not do a great deal of good in helping people heal after their losses in the war?

Blades filed the sheet of paper away and sat back. The more he thought about it, the more he was pleased about those fingerprints. Digby certainly could have hanged. What was it Digby had said? When he had been in action at the Somme the bullets had mowed down the soldiers to the left and right of him but for no reason that he could fathom left him standing and unharmed. Not unlike what Digby's experience had been in this case. His survival again seemed arbitrary.

He thought of Jean and the loss of her brother Tom. That had been devastating for her and for her family. And he did not think Jean had recovered from the pain of that yet. She was a church-goer even though her faith in the church had been damaged in the war. Their minister had preached from his pulpit to the young men there and encouraged them to do their duty by their country and by God and volunteer to fight at the Front. Because of this, she had lost her brother, as so many others had lost their young men. That had rocked her faith for some time. How could she go to her minister and her church for comfort over her loss when they'd connived in it? Yet she did. It was just of so little help. Blades had always been against her going to séances to try to get in touch with Tom, though he knew many of her friends resorted to this. When their own church had failed them, the Spiritualist church had helped. Her friends had told her it gave them the comfort of feeling that when they died, they would meet up with their loved ones on the other side. In the séances, their loved ones told them they were waiting for them. Now Blades wondered what right he had thought he had to deny Jean that comfort.

# CHAPTER FIFTY

As a church, it was small in size and simple in design, more in the style of a meeting hall than a cathedral, a stone building at least, but one that had been converted from some sort of works. The roof was low, the space restricted, but they had managed to run to a pulpit and proper pews. There was even stained glass in what had originally been a mundane, small-paned window. It now depicted a cross, amateurish in its construction but effective.

Blades and his wife were here, Blades disbelieving but Jean hopeful. Blades thought back to the telegram that her family had received; it had said that Jean's brother Tom was missing, presumed dead at the Battle of the Somme. Blades had thought this officialese unnecessarily cold, though a kind interpretation might be that the War Office thought an objective and brief use of language would make deaths easier to cope with, even if only marginally; but the bare statement was still brutal. Blades knew that Jean had found it hard to accept and that she had hoped for long enough that Tom had lost his memory, would one day recover it, and walk through the front door of the family home with a cheery grin. Because of what Blades had gleaned of life and death in the trenches, he had never thought there was hope. A lot of bodies were not identified because there was not enough left to distinguish who it might have been, and that was probably what had happened to Tom. Blades was glad when Jean eventually accepted the fact of Tom's death.

When Blades and Jean had followed the slow queue of Digby's congregation into the meeting place, Blades had noticed that the crowd was mostly female, with a lot of mothers and young wives, or sisters in it, their faces taut and anxious. Blades supposed they had all seen someone off to war, had felt the pride and dread that people did on that occasion, then suffered the agony of their not returning. He speculated on the constant letters they would have written, and the replies they would have received, brief enough in some cases where writing had been a problem for their young men, but replies there would have been, and delivery to and from the Front was quick and regular, so that the women would have known when the usual letters stopped that something had happened. To an extent, the telegram was only confirmation of what they had already worked out.

When the crowd saw the minister enter from a door on the left, their quiet whispers died away leaving an expectant silence. The minister held himself in a dignified pose as he walked in his black robe to the pulpit where he sat for a moment's prayer. The pulpit hid much of him from sight, though the movement of the top of his head as he bowed towards his clasped hands could be seen. Then there was a rustle of his vestment and he stood, his skin shining in the candles. His face was serious with office and occasion but then a smile did transpire, and Blades could see that it held forgiveness and hope, as if news of something better had reached him. The congregation stood with the organist and sang, 'Abide with me' before sitting in silence once again.

Digby stood in rapt thought in his pulpit. His eyes stared ahead of him but gave an impression that they saw nothing that was in front of them. After some time, Digby frowned and cupped his right ear with his right hand as if listening to someone standing behind his shoulder. He stood like this for a few minutes, and there was a tense silence in the congregation as they watched him.

Then he said, 'Is there a Jean here?' And the urgency and suddenness of this were electric.

Blades had not known what form Digby's communication with the dead was going to take. It came across to him as contrived, though this may have been his cynical policeman's brain. But if the question was aimed at his wife, how could Digby have known Jean's name? Blades supposed someone in Digby's position would be able to do his research but how would he have known they would come here? Blades glanced at his wife beside him; she was pale and looked at a loss.

Digby repeated, 'Is there a Jean here?'

There was urgent whispering around the meeting room, then Blades nudged Jean, and she raised a tentative hand.

The minister spoke. 'I have a message from Tom.'

Jean's reply was an exhalation of breath.

'Your brother?' the minister asked.

Digby was not in the Blades' social circle, and Blades had not expected him to know Tom's name.

'Yes.'

'He is—' and the minister hesitated. 'He says he is happy where he is. You shouldn't worry.'

Blades had Jean's hand in his now and he could feel her shake. He knew the depth of her emotions about her brother, and there was a lot of anxiety in her face as she looked towards the minister.

'Ask him—' But Jean could not bring the words out easily.

'Yes?'

'Ask him if it was quick. The telegram gave no details. I don't even know how he died.'

The minister frowned. Blades and Jean and the rest of the congregation found themselves attempting to interpret his silence. Then Digby's words were ringing out. 'It was sudden. A bullet in the chest. But he says he's at peace now.'

'Thank God.'

Then Blades felt the woman who meant most to him in the world being engulfed by sobs as tears rushed down her face. Then her head was in her hands.

An elderly woman stood up and there was desperation in her voice as she said, 'Sammy. Is our Sammy there? Please tell him to talk to us.'

The minister looked at her. 'If the dead choose to speak, they do. But I'm sorry. I can't summon them.'

'But Sammy?' the woman wailed.

Then someone else said, 'Is my Bob there?'

'And my Alfred?' another person said.

Blades looked round at the congregation and took in the pain on their faces. His hand squeezed Jean's and she returned it. There was so much desperation in this gathering of people, Blades couldn't help feeling for every one of them and, though he couldn't himself believe in all this theatre, he was glad that Jean felt she had been put in touch and been given peace.

# ACKNOWLEDGEMENTS

Thanks to the Brodie Writing Group for their
encouragement and comments.

If you enjoyed this book, please let others know by leaving a quick review on Amazon. Also, if you spot anything untoward in the paperback, get in touch. We strive for the best quality and appreciate reader feedback.

editor@thebookfolks.com

www.thebookfolks.com

35454530R00136

Printed in Poland
by Amazon Fulfillment
Poland Sp. z o.o., Wrocław